MW01134892

Shoelaces for Christmas

Shoelaces for Christmas
Craig S. Buehner

Copyright Information

For my family

Prologue

I love the holidays, and not for the gifts, bows, trees, and decorations. These things are all wonderful, but when I was a teenager, I discovered the real significance of the holidays. And as I have gotten older, the real essence of Christmas has become more evident. But the events of one Christmas, when I was fifteen, changed my life.

Chapter 1

Although I didn't realize it until I was older, I grew up in a privileged family, wanting for very little. My father was a well-respected attorney and partner in the top law firm of Godfrey, Witbeck and Miller—he was the Miller. Needless to say, we didn't struggle financially, and I usually got everything I wanted. This year, I was fully expecting a new car for Christmas, which fell just a few days before my sixteenth birthday.

Most of my friends did chores for their parents, but I never had to work around the house.

Homework was something I had to do, and I was a good student. But other than that, the majority of my time was spent playing video games and hanging out with my friends at the mall. Dad worked a lot, so he wasn't around much, although he was always home for dinner and weekends. Mom raised me and my two brothers, Nate and Mitchell.

The year this story took place, I was fifteen, Nate was twelve, and Mitchell was eight. I loved my brothers, but like most teens, I didn't get along with them very well. Mom was constantly reminding me, "James, get along with your brothers. They'll always be your family." I usually didn't listen to her lectures, but I will always remember this one. You see, family is all we have—at least all that is important. This is something most fifteen-year-old kids don't realize, and back then I didn't either. I was completely self-centered: The world revolved around me and I knew it, and I was a brat.

My attitude started to change around Halloween that year, and not for the better. It's always been one of my favorite holidays, and I always took pride in creating a costume with just the right shock value to get a lot of attention.

Mom thought I was too old to trick-or-treat, so she suggested a party instead. I threw a tantrum and demanded both. As usual, I got my way. Back then I never thought about the rotten example my behavior and rudeness to my parents was setting for my younger brothers, and I probably wouldn't have cared even if it had crossed my mind. I didn't care about anything that didn't affect me.

With Halloween just a few days away, I decided the party would start with a few hours of trick-or-treating.

Planning a party was always a big deal, but I always relied on Mom to take care of the details. All I had to do was tell my friends the time and place.

Although I was focused on Halloween, I started to notice that something was different at home. Dad started staying home a lot, and Mom seemed tired all the time. One thing I am sure of, the next few months changed my life forever.

I rarely walked home from school, but today was an exception. Mrs. Bean, my English teacher, had kept me after class to talk about my writing. She was always encouraging me to write more. My friends had all taken off, leaving me to fend for myself. I could have texted Mom, but my cell phone battery was dead, so I started walking. My house was about two miles away from my school, and I thought I would use the extra time to go over the plans for my Halloween party. The guest list was growing by the minute, and I wanted to make sure all of the cute girls showed up. I had to have something fun planned to pull that off.

The weather was still decent, warm for late autumn and a little windy, so as I walked I thought about planning a dance with a live DJ in the back yard. Lost in my thoughts, I didn't even notice when a Mercedes pulled up next to me. "You want a ride kiddo?" I recognized Dad's voice. I hated it when he called me kiddo, especially when I was with my friends. But since no one was around, I didn't make a big deal of it. I stepped off the curb and slumped into the front seat. Some boring talk radio show was coming through the speakers; I quickly turned the station.

"Hey, I was listening to that!" Dad protested.

"Dad, you drive the car—I'll drive the radio." It was my favorite line, mostly because I knew it drove him crazy. I finally found a good station and started moving to the beat. Dad didn't seem himself and seemed lost in thought. Usually he gave me more of a fight. He kept looking at me as if he wanted to say something but didn't have the words.

Dad turned onto our street and hit the button that opened the gate. I loved the sound the car tires made on our cobbled driveway, like hundreds of horses running on rocks. Dad opened the garage door and we pulled in. I quickly hopped out and headed for the door.

"James."

I didn't even turn around. "Yeah Dad?"

"Mom and I want to talk to you and your brothers tonight, so don't go far."

What? I was planning on meeting with Mike Jenson to go over the guest list and make sure everyone was going to show up for the party. His brother Joe was a DJ and we were hoping to book him for the night. I ran my hand through my hair in frustration. "But Dad, I—"

Dad looked serious. "James. Son. It's important—we need to talk to you boys." Dad's tone made me nervous. It was like he was trying to remain calm. I was afraid something horrible might be happening—like they were cancelling our cable subscription, or even worse, was our Internet going to be down? I would freak if the Internet went down. I'm in the middle of an intense game of World of Warcraft with a kid in Australia.

"Okay Dad, I'll be here."

"Thanks James. Dinner is ready. We'll talk after we eat."

I walked into the kitchen, where I was greeted with the delicious aroma of pizza. Two boxes were sitting on the countertop with the lids open, and Mitchell and Nate were already on their second slices. I grabbed a plate, piled it high, and started eating. I looked around and noticed Mom wasn't there.

"Where's Mom?" I asked.

Nate looked at me and shrugged. Mitchell was too interested in his pizza and didn't appear to hear a word.

Dad opened the door from the garage and came into the kitchen, setting his briefcase on a chair, and asked, "Well boys, are you almost done?" I had barely taken a bite. I was about to snap out a smart reply when I noticed again that something wasn't right with Dad. He looked tired and seemed agitated. I decided no response was best this time—I just shoved the pizza in my mouth and nodded.

Dad motioned for us to follow him up the stairs. He walked down the hall and entered the master bedroom. Mom was in their bed—it looked as if she had been resting there for a while. Her eyes were closed, but the red blotches around them made it obvious she had been crying. Dad looked at her with concern as he reached out to touch her shoulder.

She opened her eyes and smiled at us. "Boys, how was school?" she asked, exhaustion evident in her voice. She pulled herself up, and Dad placed a couple of pillows behind her shoulders so she would be more comfortable.

I was becoming a little anxious now. Mom liked to stay active and healthy, but something told me her exhaustion was more than a little flu bug. Dad sat on the end of the bed. It looked as if he was trying to pick the right words, which was strange—as an attorney finding the right words was usually easy for him. After several moments he started to talk.

"Mom and I have something we need to tell you—" Tears welled up in his eyes. Never in my life had I seen my father cry. I wasn't sure if he was even capable of crying. My heart started to pound.

"What Dad? Just say it," I demanded, a little more harshly than I'd meant to speak.

It took another moment for Dad to compose himself, but finally he did. "I don't know if you've noticed, but I've been home more lately helping Mom." Mom had been in her room more than usual but I just figured she needed her rest or had the flu—something like that.

"I've noticed." I was anxious now, and wanted Dad to get to the point. "What's going on?" Mom started talking. "I need you boys to promise you won't freak out, okay?" We all nodded as a tear trickled down her cheek.

"Just tell us what's going on!" I demanded again. I was freaking out, despite what I had just promised Mom. She looked at me and smiled. "Boys, I'm sick. I have a rare form of cancer that is affecting my bones."

"Cancer? How can you have cancer?" I asked, as my fear gave way to anger. Cancer was only supposed to affect other people, not my mom. I felt like someone had reached in my chest and pulled out my heart. I could feel the tears welling up—I quickly tried to blink them away. Nate started to cry, and Mitchell, as usual, seemed oblivious.

"Boys, it's okay," Mom said calmly. "I'm going to the hospital tomorrow to have surgery. The doctors are hoping they can remove the affected tissues and then I'll be okay. We didn't want to scare you, but we wanted to let you know. Going to the hospital for surgery is a big deal—we want to make sure you boys understand what's going on."

I didn't know what to say or do. I should have just kept my mouth shut, but instead I said something I will regret for the rest of my life. "So does this mean I can't have my party?" I asked.

Judging from the look Dad gave me I had my answer. I also saw the disappointment on his face. I quickly tried to explain what I was trying to say. "I mean…I'm sure you don't want a lot of people…well…." I realized how selfish this sounded, but it was as if I couldn't stop myself.

Mom put her hand on mine and smiled, "I know how much you are looking forward to the party, but the surgery is going to wear me out. I've already discussed the possibility of moving the party to Mike's house, and his mother agreed. I hope that's okay with you."

It didn't matter now. I felt terrible about what I had said. She could have told me the party was going to be held on the moon and I wouldn't have cared.

"Listen James, I know this doesn't play out with your plans. We didn't plan for this either. But here we are. Please understand, after the surgery I will be in bed for a while," Mom continued.

"No, Mom it's okay…I'm sorry, I didn't mean to…"

"Don't worry James, it will be okay."

"You promise?"

"I promise." Dad shot Mom a look. Mom just winked back.

Clearly there was something else going on—something they didn't want to tell us. I could see it in the way they were looking at each other. I decided to keep that thought to myself. I didn't want to ask, didn't want to know. I was having a rare moment of compassion, and I really didn't want to scare my little brothers.

"We have to leave early," Dad said. "Grandma is on her way over. She's going to sit with you boys tonight. We won't be here when you wake up for school, so make sure you do what she says. I'll pick you up after school and we'll go visit Mom in the hospital."

All we could do was agree; we didn't have a choice. I felt my phone vibrating in my pocket. I pulled it out and looked at the screen. Mike was calling, most likely to discuss the change of venue for the party. Suddenly I didn't care. I clicked ignore and put the phone back in my pocket.

Chapter 2

I was counting down the minutes until the final bell rang. I had so much going through my mind it was hard to concentrate on school. I just wanted to leave. Dad was picking us up to go see Mom. The bell finally rang, and I packed up and headed for the front of the school. Dad's car was at the curb. I ran down and hopped in the front passenger seat. Nate and Mitchell were already in the back—Dad must have checked them out of school early. We started toward the hospital, just a few blocks away.

Dad didn't say much on the ride over, other than that the surgery was over and Mom was recovering. He hadn't had a chance to speak with the doctor, so he wasn't sure how things had gone.

We rode the elevator up to the third floor and walked straight to room 311. Mom was lying in the bed, hooked to an assortment of tubes and wires connected to a monitor that beeped steadily. A nurse sat nearby, typing information into a computer. "Mr. Miller, I'm glad you're back. Jan hasn't awakened yet," the nurse said as we arrived.

"It's been a while. Is that normal?" Dad asked.

"Yes. Her body is exhausted. She may not be alert until morning." The nurse started to walk out the door but turned around at the threshold. "The doctor will be back shortly. He would like to speak with you."

"Good. I want to talk to him too," Dad replied.

I looked at Mom—she looked frail. I had never seen Mom in a hospital, at least not because she was sick. I visited when each of my brothers were born, but that wasn't anything like this. I felt sick to my stomach. I wanted to cry, but tears didn't come. I hated seeing her like this and wanted to get out of there. Maybe it was selfish, but I didn't want to come back either.

"Mr. Miller." We both turned to see Dr. Lewis walk into the room.

"Yes doctor, how did everything go?" Dad offered his hand to Dr. Lewis, who shook Dad's hand and quietly asked if they could speak in the hallway.

Dad followed him out; Dr. Lewis shut the door behind them. I couldn't help thinking that couldn't be a good sign. Why couldn't he talk in front of us? Was the news that bad? They were gone for what seemed like forever. I didn't dare walk into the hall for fear of hearing something I wasn't ready for.

But at the same time, I didn't want to wait in the room any longer because I couldn't stand to see Mom lying there. I heard a noise coming from the hospital bed—I turned to see Mom moving. Quickly I walked to her. Mom's eyes fluttered open and she looked at me. She smiled and tried to speak, but nothing came out. She closed her eyes and seemed to fall asleep again.

I heard the door open as Dad came back into the room. "She woke up!" I exclaimed.

"She did? When?" Dad asked.

"Just now. Right before you came back!" I said.

Dad walked over to Mom and placed his hand on hers. She didn't react as he sat down in the chair to her. I didn't like the look on his face—he was obviously concerned. I wanted to ask what the doctor said, but I figured he would tell us when he was ready.

My stomach started to growl. It must have been loud enough for Dad to hear because he said he wanted to take us to the hospital cafeteria for dinner.

"Let's go eat and we'll come back and check on Mom later," he said. We agreed, and headed for the elevator.

We returned to the room to find Mom awake and talking to the nurse. She still seemed groggy, but she smiled when she saw us walk in.

"How are you guys?" she asked slowly.

"Good!" we all answered in unison.

Dad walked to her side. The nurse looked up and asked, "Did Dr. Lewis speak with you?"

"He did," Dad answered. "I want to talk to Jan, but I think we'll take her home. She'll be more comfortable there."

Mom looked at him, appearing hurt. He caught her gaze and in that moment they communicated a thousand words. The outlook wasn't good. The surgery didn't work.

"What? Is she okay? Is she going to be alright?" I was speaking through tears. But I knew from the look in Dad's eyes things were bad.

"James—" Just the way Mom said my name told me I didn't want to hear any more. Through my tears I felt my emotions again spiraling out of control. I was sad, and really angry. I wasn't sure who to blame, so I blamed them.

"You lied to me. You promised me things would be okay. YOU PROMISED!" I shouted.

Mom stretched out her hand, "James, listen—" I didn't want to listen. I didn't want to hear any more. I turned and ran into the hallway toward the elevator. I could hear Dad calling after me. There were several people waiting for the elevator, so I found the stairs. I stormed down to the main floor and headed for the front doors.

Tears were streaming down my face—my mind was reeling. How could this be happening to me? I kept running until I hit the street. I wasn't sure where I was going, but I knew I couldn't stay there another minute. My cell phone vibrated in my pocket and I slowed down enough to look at the screen. It displayed, "Dad Incoming Call." I hit the ignore button and kept running.

I was headed for the city center as night was falling. The temperatures easily drop to freezing this time of the year, and my lungs ached from breathing the cold air. My legs ached too, but I couldn't stop moving. The streets were crowded with people heading home for the day.

As I continued running through town, I noticed a change in the people I was passing on the streets.

In the shopping districts, everyone was dressed nicely and seemed to move purposefully. But the people I saw now were wearing dirty clothes, many sitting on the curbs, some drinking from paper bags. Others huddled into ill-fitting coats and hugged themselves for warmth.

A sign on the building I ran past read, "Donate blood and receive $20." I stumbled over a man digging through a garbage can and realized I had never been to this part of town. The fear that had driven me from the hospital was suddenly replaced by terror. Now I didn't want to stop—not in this neighborhood—but I was worn out. By now I had easily run three miles. My lungs were on fire and my legs finally faltered. I stopped in front of an old building with a sign out front— FAMILY SAFE HAVEN.

"Hey buddy, you got a light?" I was jolted from my thoughts by a thin, poorly dressed man with a scruffy beard. He stood directly in front of me, waving a cigarette. "Uh…No…Sorry, I don't think I do," I said quickly. The man gave me a funny look and walked away. A woman who appeared to be about Mom's age was standing at the front door to the old building. She seemed to be dressed better than most of the other people who were hanging around. Her soft eyes were covered with glasses, and she smiled warmly at me as she moved surely and quickly to my side.

"Can I help you son?" she asked.

"No…I mean—" I stammered.

"Are you lost?" she asked.

"No not exactly," I said.

"What brings you down here?" she continued.

"Well I was at the hospital, but—" I began, but she interrupted. "Hospital? Are you sick? Wait a minute. You look familiar. Is Spencer Miller your father?"

"Um, yes," I said cautiously.

"Oh, I recognize you from the picture your father just showed me. He's been looking for you. Does he know you're here?" she asked.

"Well no…not exactly," I answered, looking away.

"Come in, I'll give him a call." She turned toward the building, her hand on my elbow.

"NO! I mean…I don't want to talk with him, at least not now," I said.

"Don't you think he's worried? Why don't I call him? I'll ask if you can stay and help us for a few hours," she answered.

Help who? I didn't want to help anyone. I didn't want to do anything. I wanted to find a park bench and just sit by myself. My mind was protesting, but my mouth said, "Sure, I guess that would be fine."

"My name is Ruth," she said, offering her hand. As I took her hand, I answered, "I'm James."

"Nice to meet you James," Ruth said, gripping my hand hard.

Ruth pulled out her phone and dialed Dad's number. After a few seconds she said, "Hi Spencer. Yes, fine thanks. I just wanted to let you know I have your son here. Yes, James, he's here. Well I see…Okay, but I have an idea—leave him here with us for a few hours. I'll keep him busy. Great, it's settled then—see you at ten."

Ruth clicked the phone off. "Perfect. Now come on in so I can introduce you to a few people."

I followed Ruth, more than a little worried about what I had gotten myself into. We walked through a kitchen where

20

several people were working. A large dishwasher in the middle of the room was completely surrounded by shelves of dishes, stacked high. We entered a large cafeteria with a long table extending the length of one wall. Empty warming plates and platters were scattered across the table, and a man was working at clearing them away. The rest of the room was filled with tables and chairs. It looked as if dinner was mostly finished for the night, although a few people lingered, slowly eating soup. Everyone I saw was wearing worn out clothes that didn't seem to fit very well. Many looked like they were in need of a shower.

Suddenly I remembered Dad talking about Family Safe Haven; he had called it a homeless shelter for families. Dad's law firm held an annual golf tournament to raise money for it. Last year he let me play on his team.

I followed Ruth down a long hall and into a room filled with kids of all ages. Several tables were covered with cards and game boards. A few toddlers were digging through toy boxes. Two TVs were set up in a corner, each with a separate game system. A bookshelf next to the television was loaded with games, but most of their cases were worn and tattered. Two teenage boys about my age were playing Ping-Pong.

I noticed a little girl about five or six sitting alone on a chair in the corner, staring at the wall in front of her as if she were waiting for it to move. She was the only kid in the room who wasn't playing. I wondered if she was in trouble, and was sitting in time-out or something like that. Ruth must have noticed. "So what do you think James? Do you have any questions for me?"

I had many questions, like why was I even here? I didn't belong. I just wanted to leave. "Where are their parents?" I asked instead.

"Good question. Everyone here is homeless for one reason or another. We are a family shelter and our goal is to help them get back on their feet. Most of the parents are in training classes to help them find jobs. The rest are in AA meetings or drug rehabilitation classes. Because of the family structure of the shelter, there are no drugs or alcohol allowed— their use is prohibited. If someone is addicted, we help them get clean," Ruth answered.

I wasn't really listening to Ruth; I didn't really care. This had nothing to do with my mom. I continued watching the little girl in the corner, and I couldn't help wondering what her story was.

Somehow she looked different from the rest of the kids. Maybe it was just because she was by herself. I wasn't sure if I should ask about her or not—so I didn't.

"You told my dad I would stay and help. What do you want me to do?" I asked uncomfortably.

"I want you to hang out with the kids. They don't get to hang out with kids from normal family situations. I think it would be good for them." Ruth looked at me over the rim of her glasses. "I also think it might be good for you."

Good for me? Whatever! I felt completely out of place and decided I would rather go home than hang out with a bunch of strangers. Just as I pulled out my cell phone to ask my dad to come get me, the little girl looked over at me, but quickly turned back to the wall. I put my phone back in my pocket.

"What's up with her?" I finally asked pointing to the girl.

"Well, she's a sweet little girl, but she keeps to herself. She never talks. I don't think I have ever heard her say a word," Ruth answered.

"Why?"

"We're not sure. Her mom was addicted to drugs when they first arrived. We helped her through rehab while Chloe stayed with us," Ruth said.

"That's her name? Chloe?" I asked.

"Yes. She and her mom lived on the streets for a while and I think that affected her. While her mom was strung out on drugs, Chloe was neglected. When they came to us it was obvious she hadn't eaten in a while. Physically, she's doing great, but mentally—only time will tell," Ruth said.

"Where's her mom now?" I asked.

"She does odd jobs. Currently she cleans office buildings at night. She'll be back soon." Ruth's comment made me think about my own mom. She had never neglected me. She'd always been there for me and made sure I got everything I ever wanted, even when I didn't really want her around. I wondered what it would be like if Mom wasn't there? Thoughts like that made me sick, so I turned my attention back to Chloe, who was still staring at the wall. I understood how she felt.

I had heard enough. To me, this place was horrible and I didn't like the smell. I was ready to go home. I pulled my phone from my pocket again and sent a text to Dad.

"I'm sure George and Grant over there would love to let you join in a game of Ping-Pong," Ruth said.

"No thanks, I'm good. I just texted my dad. He'll be here soon," I answered.

Ruth's smile disappeared like I had said something wrong. "Okay, but come visit us again, would you? We can always use extra help." The disappointment in her voice was obvious.

"Yeah, sure," I said, without meaning it.

I walked past her trying to find my way out. Eventually I found the exit and walked out onto the sidewalk. The sun had gone down by then, which made the street look even scarier than when I had first arrived. I just wanted to get out of there. A few moments later Dad pulled up in the Mercedes. I jumped in and we drove off.

Chapter 3

Dad and I didn't speak on the way back. I didn't even bother with the radio. I wasn't sure if we were heading back to the hospital or going home. I wanted to ask if Mom was coming home, but I sat silent instead.

Dad wasn't happy—I thought for sure he would say something about the shelter, but he didn't. I knew his thoughts were elsewhere, and he was probably irritated that he had to leave Mom to come get me. I wondered if he was going to spend the night in the hospital with Mom or relieve Grandma so she didn't have to stay with us at the house. He pulled up to our driveway, slowing while the gate opened.

"Your brothers are inside with Grandma. I'll see you in the morning." There wasn't much emotion in his voice as he stopped in front of the house.

"Where are you going?" I asked, as if I didn't know.

"Back to be with Mom. See you in the morning." I watched him drive away. I knew I shouldn't have run off, but I didn't care. I just wanted to go inside and forget everything. I wanted to play World of Warcraft with my friend in Australia.

I walked into the house to find Nate and Mitchell fighting over the computer.

"It's my turn!" Nate yelled.

"You just had it for 20 minutes. It's my turn!" Mitchell hollered back.

"Actually, it's my turn, so the two of you can find something else to do," I intervened.

"What makes you think you get a turn?" Nate asked in disgust.

"First of all, the computer is mine, and second, it's early afternoon in Sydney, so my Australian friend is online."

"It's not yours—you always say it's yours."

"It is mine. I got it for Christmas. The package was closest to my gifts, which makes it mine."

"The tag on the package said, To The Boys."

"No, it said To The Boy, and that's me. I'm the oldest, making me THE boy. Now get out of here."

They drove me crazy. Mom says I should try harder to get along with them, but it's impossible.

Grandma must have heard us because she stormed into the room and shut off the TV.

"Hey! What did you do that for?" I asked, becoming even more irritated.

"I'm not going to sit here and listen to you boys argue for another minute. It's ridiculous that you can't get along. Go up to your rooms." Grandma raised her voice, which was something she rarely did. My brothers immediately headed upstairs. I stayed put, pleased she had sent them away so I could start my game.

"You too mister!" she said sternly.

"Oh c'mon, I have a time slot I have to play!" I didn't like being told what to do, especially by someone who wasn't my mom or dad.

"You can play tomorrow. Go upstairs."

"NO!" I shouted angrily. I'd had enough of everything that day; I wasn't going to take any more.

Grandma seemed stunned by my outburst.

"Listen James. Your mother is gravely sick in the hospital and I think you might show a little respect by helping out around here," she said.

That was the last straw. "What do you know about anything?" I said loudly. "Mom promised she would be fine and she lied, so why should I have to do anything to help out now? Besides, she cares more about everyone else than she does about us anyway. Just the other day she made a plate of cookies. Did she offer me one? No, she took the whole plate to the neighbors. She didn't save anything for her own family." I was on a roll now. It was like all my pent-up frustration was running out of my mouth with no filter.

"Are you done?" Grandma asked, disappointment evident in her voice.

"No, as a matter of fact I'm not," I continued. "A few weeks ago I came home and she was cooking dinner. I asked when we could eat, and she said our dinner was on the stove. Do you know what she did? She pointed to a pot of stew. That's right, a pot of stew. She said the stew was for us and the other amazing dinner was going to a family down the street. They ate the good stuff while we ate the slop. And now she's sick. I have a party in a few days and I can't even have it here. She's too tired to—"

"ENOUGH!" Grandma yelled, interrupting my tirade. From the look on her face, I could tell I had definitely said too much.

"Your mother is a wonderful person and if you don't realize that, you're a fool. She was taking those meals to neighbors who were sick—people who needed help. And do you know what the best part is?" I just sat there staring at Grandma, shocked. I couldn't believe she was yelling at me. "Well, do you?"

"No, but I bet you're going to tell me," I answered rudely.

"You're darn right I'm going to tell you. No one asked her to do any of those things. She did them out of the kindness of her heart. And she did it while she was sick herself. If you have a problem with that, and you can't see her for who she is, then you are a selfish brat who doesn't know his own mother."

I just sat there stunned. I knew I should have told her I didn't mean it, but I was still too angry.

Nothing was happening the way it was supposed to. Grandma shouldn't be here and Mom should be upstairs in her own room. I didn't even say a word; I just turned and walked away.

"Don't come back down either!" She hollered after me.

"Don't worry, I won't!" I stomped up the stairs and turned to walk down the hall. Nate was standing there, staring at me.

"What was that all about?" he asked.

"Don't worry about it. It's not a big deal, not a big deal at all," I said sarcastically as I strolled off to my room. I opened my door and walked in, slamming the door behind me. I walked over and sat on the edge of my bed. I wasn't proud of what just happened, but I couldn't take it back now. Grandma was right—I didn't really appreciate Mom. I took her for granted. I didn't think that much about why she did things, and I'd never had any reason to wonder before now. I lay down on my back looking up at my ceiling; I closed my eyes and the world went black.

Chapter 4

I woke up to the morning sun streaming through my window. I stood up and walked into the bathroom and looked in the mirror. My hair was standing straight up and I had an indent in my face from sleeping on my sleeve. I looked as terrible as I felt. As I stood staring at my reflection I heard a knock at the door.

"It's open!" I yelled. I thought for sure it would be Grandma wanting to go another round.

"Hey!" Through the reflection in the mirror I saw Dad walk in the door.

"Hi," I said back, almost shamefully.

"Can we talk?"

Like I had a choice. "Sure, about what?"

"I heard you had a little conversation with Grandma last night."

I suddenly realized that I probably wasn't going to like this talk.

"Yeah, about that…"

Dad cut me off. "Son, just so you know, I'm not going to tell Mom about your talk with Grandma.

She's promised not to say anything as well because we both agree telling Mom won't solve anything.

"My concern is you."

"Me? What did I do?"

"James, you're fifteen years old. Soon you'll be sixteen. It's time to grow up. You need to start showing me you can be responsible," Dad said.

"I am responsible," I answered quickly.

"For what? You don't do anything," he said.

"I help! I do things!" I shot back. I knew it wasn't really true, but I felt myself getting angry anyway.

I raised my voice but I didn't want to get into an argument with Dad too. Besides, I knew I would lose.

"Okay, you do things every once in a while. But I want you to learn real responsibility," he continued.

I thought about it for a moment. "So what did you have in mind?" I asked nervously.

"Did I tell you you're getting a car for Christmas?"

"Yes you did," I answered. Of course I knew! We'd even gone to the showroom to check them out.

"So here's my plan. Having your own car requires a tremendous amount of responsibility. You have to change the oil, put gas in the tank, make sure it stays clean, and keep it licensed and insured.

I'm going to help with those things, but you are the one responsible for doing them," Dad began.

I liked where this was going. Learning responsibility by having a car. Dad was a genius. But then he continued. "You need to show me you can be responsible before you get the car. If that means we wait a year, so be it."

I stared at him, disbelief all over my face. How could he do this to me? He'd promised me a car! I decided to play it cool—at least long enough to see where he was going with this.

"What do you have in mind?" I asked cautiously.

"It's already been arranged. You're going to work one day a week with Ruth," Dad said.

"But—" I started to protest, but Dad cut me off. "That's not all. You're going to work one day a week at home as well."

"At home? Doing what?" I asked.

"Whatever your mom asks you to do," he said.

I had to think quickly. There was no way I was going to work all day at either place. Suddenly it came to me. "School." I smacked the sink with my palm. "What about school?"

"You'll work after school two days a week. One day here at home and the other with Ruth at the homeless shelter." Dad had a resolve in his voice that told me to get used to the idea, because there was no getting out of it. If I wanted my car, this was the way it would be.

"How long do I have to work before I can get the car?" I asked, resigned.

"Good question. Your mom and I will decide if you've done a good job around the house, and display perfect respect for her and your brothers along with your chores. And I'll meet with Ruth a few days before Christmas to see how you are doing there," Dad answered.

All the way until Christmas? I was fuming. Dad had already promised me a car—it was supposed to be a gift, not something I had to earn. But I figured going along with his plan was best—for now.

"Fine. When do I start?" I mumbled.

"Tomorrow."

"Okay then—wait—my party. Tomorrow is Halloween!" I exclaimed.

Dad lifted an eyebrow. "Perfect! They have a lot of fun with the kids at the shelter on Halloween."

"But I have the coolest costume for the party," I protested.

"You can wear it to the shelter," he said.

"This stinks! You know I've been planning this party for weeks," I grumbled.

"Wrong! You have been looking forward to the party for weeks. Your mother has been planning it.

Anyway, you can go after. The shelter wraps things up at nine," Dad said.

That wasn't so bad. The party started at eight and would go 'til midnight. That would give me a few good hours at least. I didn't want to give in too easily, so I thought about it for a while longer.

"Okay. I'll start tomorrow," I agreed.

"Perfect! I knew you would see things my way." Dad stood up and walked toward the door. Just before he left he said, "By the way, Mom is coming home this afternoon."

I paused. "Is she okay?"

Dad sighed. "For now son. We're taking it one day at a time."

Halloween morning—this was going to be a great day! As I walked down the stairs Mom was up making breakfast. I was surprised! She looked great and seemed energetic as she cooked potatoes and pancakes. I sat down at the counter.

"Good morning," she said cheerfully.

"You look like you're feeling better." I couldn't believe that even though she was sick, she was still up making breakfast for us.

"Well the doctor said there would be good days and bad. Today's a good day, so I decided to embrace it. Do you want pancakes?" She turned around with her spatula and flipped two pancakes onto a plate. I hadn't even answered before she set the plate in front of me.

"Sure, sounds good. Please pass the syrup?"

Mom put butter and syrup in front of me. It had been a long time since she'd cooked breakfast.

She's a great cook and her pancakes are the best.

"So are you going to the party tonight?" she asked, returning to the griddle.

"Yeah, right after the shelter," I answered.

"The shelter?" she asked.

Dad hadn't told her! Was this part of the plan? Did he want to see if I would tell her about our little deal, or was this a test? I decided to treat it as a test.

"Yeah, I decided to volunteer at the shelter tonight helping the kids." I was playing it cool. She didn't need to know I was tricked into it.

She looked surprised. A tear trickled from her eye. "That's wonderful James. I think that's a great thing for you to do. Are any of your friends going with you?"

I thought, that's not a bad idea. I'm sure I could get a few of them to go. Some of my friends seem to like to help out when it's for a good cause. "Nope, just me," I said.

"Oh honey, that makes it even better. I have always hoped that you would learn how great it feels to help others. I'm so proud of you."

She walked over and gave me a hug—something I wasn't expecting. I hadn't hugged my mom in a long time. It was nice, and it felt good to think she was proud of me.

Dad walked into the kitchen and sat down at the table.

"Did you hear what your son is doing today? He's volunteering at the shelter!" Mom exclaimed.

I winked at Dad. He saw how I was playing this and smiled back at me. "That's great son. I think that's just great."

"Thanks Dad. Can I get a ride there after school?"

Dad looked up at me with a sly grin. "You know, I have a meeting today. When were you planning on going?"

"After school," I repeated.

"Yeah, no—I can't take you," he said, opening the newspaper.

"How do you expect me to get there if you don't drive me?" I asked, confused.

The way he started I knew he had planned this all along. "Well, a responsible person like you is very resourceful. I'm sure you can figure out a way," he said.

I looked at Mom. "Don't look at me," she said. "I'm not allowed to drive yet. But there is public transportation."

Were they actually suggesting I take the bus? I couldn't take the bus. What would my friends say? I didn't even know how to ride the bus!

"I have never taken the bus," I protested. "I don't even know where to get on. Does it stop on the corner?"

"Yeah, city buses generally stop on the corner. You know, under the little blue signs on the street," Dad answered.

"Little blue signs? I've never noticed little blue signs," I said.

"There's usually a bench under the sign. Haven't you noticed people sitting on the bench waiting for the bus?" he asked. I looked at him blankly. "Never mind, you'll figure it out," Dad said, trying not to laugh.

He carried his plate to the sink and started to walk out, but quickly turned around. "Oh, by the way—the bus costs money."

What? You have to pay to ride the bus? I thought it was public transportation—doesn't that mean it's free? I wondered how much money I would have to fork out for my bus ride.

"How much?" I asked, now feeling edgy and defensive.

"I have no idea—I don't ride the bus," Dad said with a mischievous smile. He loved this. I felt like he was just waiting for me to fail.

After Dad left the kitchen, Mom said, "I'll make sure he picks you up so you can get to at least some of the party."

I managed a smile. "Thanks Mom."

Mom kissed me on the cheek, "I hear Kristy O'Neil is going to be there."

Where did she get this stuff? I've had a crush on Kristy for months now. I didn't even know Kristy was going to the party, so how did Mom know?

"Where did you hear that?" I asked, blushing.

"You do realize that all of the Moms talk?" Mom said.

Oh man—so all the moms know? It made me sick to think all of my friend's mothers talking about me. She looked at the clock on the wall. "You better get going—I don't want you to be late for school."

I headed out the door. As Mike picked me up, my last thought as we left the curb was, "I can't believe my mom knows about Kristy O'Neil."

Chapter 5

The bell rang and I ran from my class. I had looked up the bus schedule on my phone. Bus #511 picked up outside the school and stopped near the Family Safe Haven, and I didn't want to miss it. I only had a few minutes to get to the bus stop. I was dodging kids in the hallway as I ran to the front doors. I heard a hall monitor yell for me to slow down, but I ignored him. If I missed the bus I'd have to wait 45 minutes for the next one.

I ran out onto the steps in front of the school. I could see the bus approaching, and I ran faster. The bus started to slow down. A woman was sitting on the bench, waiting for the same bus. I was relieved—I should have enough time. I got in line behind the woman and followed her onto the bus. She put a bill into a machine next to the driver. I stepped up and asked, "How much?"

"One dollar," the driver replied.

I pulled a dollar bill from my pocket and fed the machine. I walked down the aisle and found a seat across from the woman who had gotten on before me.

The bus made several stops, with people getting off and on along the route to downtown.

As we got closer to the shelter, I suddenly felt a wave of anxiety. I didn't know how to signal the driver to pull over, and

I knew my stop was coming up quickly. I looked out the front of the bus and could see the Family Safe Haven. I started to panic. I didn't know if I should stand up and holler or run to the front—I hadn't been paying attention to how the other stops had been signaled. Luckily, the woman across from me reached up and pulled the cord above her head. A bell sounded and the bus began to slow, and stopped about 30 feet from the entrance of the shelter. I let the woman get off first, and I followed.

Ruth was standing in the doorway—I figured she was waiting for me. The woman walked up to Ruth and smiled. Ruth asked, "Did you have a nice day?" She just nodded and walked in. "James!"

Ruth exclaimed as if she was excited to see me. I was still trying to figure out Ruth. Was she really that nice or was it an act?

"Hi Ruth," I said back to her.

"Are you ready for today?" she asked.

"Not really," I shrugged. "I guess it depends on what we're doing."

"Well to start, you're going to help in the kitchen."

The kitchen? Oh great, this was going to be fun. "What do you want me to do?" I asked.

"I want you to help serve dinner to our guests."

"Guests?" Ruth made it sound like this was a hotel and she was the maître d'.

"Of course they're guests. This isn't a permanent arrangement. As soon as they're ready, they move out—hopefully into something more stable. That makes them guests," she explained.

I couldn't argue with that.

Ruth turned and walked into the shelter, stopping at a closet, "You'll find an apron in there. I suggest you wear one. I don't want you to ruin your nice school clothes." I opened the door and saw several aprons hanging from a rod. I picked through them trying to find something that was at least partially clean. I put the apron over my shoulder and followed Ruth.

"Now you're going to serve soup. We don't have an endless supply, so everyone gets one scoop—except for the young kids—they get half a scoop. If they eat everything in their bowl and still want more, they can come back through," she explained.

"Sounds easy," I nodded.

"Oh, it is sweetie, but if someone gets upset because they only got one scoop—stand your ground. Don't give them more. If we gave everyone all they wanted, we would run out," she said.

"So, what am I supposed to do if someone freaks out?" I asked.

"Just ask one of the staff. They'll help calm things down," she assured me. "It doesn't happen very often, unless someone is new." That didn't make me feel better.

A woman passed by with a large pot of soup and headed for the dining room. She set it on a long table that ran along the wall and placed a ladle next to it. As she walked back she turned to me and said, "Five minutes and we start." I suddenly had a flashback to grade school. She reminded me of one of the lunch ladies who worked in the kitchen at my elementary school.

"You'd better get your apron on so you're ready," Ruth told me as she turned and walked out. I tied the apron around my neck and walked over to where the pot was sitting. I picked up the ladle and just stared at it. What was I doing here? I looked out the windows and saw a line forming on the sidewalk outside.

Several other people walked out of the kitchen and joined me along the table. Tonight's menu included cream of broccoli soup, tossed green salad, and a roll. There was a large cooler at the end of the table with cups neatly stacked next to it.

"Are we ready?" Ruth asked with a loud voice.

The woman next to me who was serving rolls said, "Let 'em in!"

Ruth unlocked the door. People started walking toward us—picking up a bowl and utensils as they made their way down the table. There were people of all ages and races. I was growing more uncomfortable by the minute; I had never been around homeless people before. I kept telling myself, I'm doing this for a car. That seemed to help a little, but not much.

The first man caught me off guard. "I pl'z has zoop?"

"Umm…Sorry, what was that?" I couldn't understand a word he said. His accent was strong; I couldn't tell where it was from.

"Zoop sonny, I want zoop." I got it that time. I scooped up a ladle full and filled his bowl.

"Thanks much, sa."

I just shook my head. This was going to be a long night. The constant flow of people never seemed to subside. I started to run out of soup and didn't know what to do. Should I turn people away? I was saved by one of the workers who brought out a fresh pot. I was relieved and upset at the same time—relieved that I wouldn't have to turn people away, but upset because I had to stand there longer.

After another half hour or so I could see the end of the line. I could see Chloe standing with the woman from the bus. The woman was pretty, dressed in a long-sleeved sweater and worn jeans. Her long, chestnut hair was pulled back into a ponytail. As they got closer I looked at Chloe. "Do you

want some soup?" I asked. She just stared at me.

"She doesn't say much. In fact, she doesn't talk at all anymore," the woman from the bus said. She was polite and seemed very nice.

"I'm sorry, I didn't mean anything. I was just saying—"

"No, it's fine. I just didn't want you to be offended when she didn't answer. Chloe would love a bowl of soup."

I scooped half a ladle and poured it in her bowl. "Do you think she wants more? She can have more if she wants."

"No, that's perfect. Thank you."

The woman held out her bowl and I poured a full ladle for her.

"Thank you so much," she said as she pushed Chloe farther on down the line.

"You're welcome," I responded. Chloe's mom wasn't at all what I had pictured. She didn't look like a recovering drug addict. Of course, my Mom didn't look like she had cancer. I wondered how old Chloe was.

"Excuse me, ma'am," I said before the woman had gone too far.

She turned to look at me. "Yes?"

"How old is Chloe?"

The woman smiled. "She's nine."

"Nine?" I said surprised.

"I know—she's short for her age. She looks like she's six." I didn't know what to say, so I just smiled and nodded as they left to find a seat at one of the tables. I felt drawn to Chloe, but I didn't know exactly why. I wondered why she didn't talk. I was still watching them when Ruth came up and stood next to me.

"Good work tonight James," she said.

"Thanks Ruth, am I done?" I asked.

"Yes, you can go. Your dad is waiting out front," she said.

I quickly took the apron off and tried to hand it to Ruth.

"That goes back where you found it," she said, smiling.

I started to walk toward the closet, but paused to turn and look at Ruth. "That woman over there with Chloe—"

"Charlotte?"

"Is that her name?" I asked.

"Yes it is, what about her?" Ruth said.

"Is she Chloe's mom?" I asked.

"She is," Ruth answered. "Beautiful isn't she?"

I wasn't going to say that, but it was true. Instead I said, "You told me the other night she was

strung out on drugs."

"I know, sad isn't it? But she's clean now and doing great. That's what we do here James. We help

people like Charlotte," Ruth explained.

I was starting to feel a little different about the shelter. It still smelled bad, and most of the people still scared me— they were so different from everything I had ever known—but I was starting to feel more comfortable around them. I was beginning to like Ruth, too. I would never tell her that, but it was obvious she really cared about people. She reminded me of my mom. Grandma was right; Mom helped people in her own way, just like Ruth. I turned and headed for the front door.

"Thanks, have a good night," Ruth called after me. I just waved my hand in the air behind me. I walked out onto the sidewalk and saw Dad's Mercedes waiting next to the curb. I got into the car and he pulled out into traffic.

"So, how was it?" Dad asked.

I didn't want him to know that it was actually okay. I just wanted to do my duty and get my car.

Ruth thought I did well and that was where Dad would get his information anyway.

"Great. It was just great." I tried to be as sarcastic as possible. At this point I was just looking forward to the party. "Will you drop me off at Mike's?"

"Don't you want to go home and change first?" Dad asked.

"Not really, why?" I said.

"Because you have soup hardened on your shirt. Didn't you wear an apron?" Dad laughed.

"Of course I wore an apron." I looked down and couldn't believe how much soup I'd managed to spill on my shirt.

Dad just shook his head. "Rookie."

Dad stopped at home and I ran in to change. Mom was sitting on the sofa, reading a book. "How was the shelter?" she asked.

"Tell you about it later." I flashed her a smile as I rushed past.

She smiled back and said, "Oh yes, of course, the party. Did you serve the meal or wear it?"

"Apparently both," I said lightly.

"Throw your shirt in the laundry room. I'll spray it with some stain remover when I go upstairs," she offered.

"Thanks Mom," I said. I quickly did what she asked and put on a new shirt. I changed my jeans as well, just for good measure. I wanted to look good for Kristy.

Dad was patiently waiting in the car for me. I hopped in the passenger seat and we were off.

"I bet you can't wait for me to drive so you don't have to play taxi," I said hopefully.

Dad smiled. "We'll see," he said, and then drove in silence to the party. As we pulled up I could see Kristy standing at the top of the drive with Mike. I got out quickly and Dad sped off.

Chapter 6

"Mike, what's up?" I said coolly.

"Nothing dude, just waiting for you," he answered.

Kristy giggled, "Hi James!"

I felt tongue-tied. I couldn't get anything out. Finally I mustered back, "Hi Kristy." I felt like an idiot, but she was so beautiful. Her hair was usually curly, but tonight it was straight, just over her shoulders. I loved it that way. I was hoping for some alone time with her, but I had barely worked up the nerve to say hi. Mike would know what to do—he's kissed several girls. I'd never even held a girl's hand. What a loser!

"Do you want to go in?" Kristy asked.

"Umm…Sure! That sounds—"

She surprised me by grabbing my hand and giving it a squeeze. We walked hand-in-hand toward the front door. I turned to look at Mike; he had a cheesy grin on his face and gave me a thumbs up.

We went to the punch bowl and I took cups and poured us punch. I'd been serving all night, but this was different. I handed her a cup.

"Thanks James, you're such a gentleman," she said sweetly.

Just then, I noticed everyone in the room was wearing costumes, which reminded me—"Crap!" I exclaimed.

"What's wrong?" Kristy asked.

"I forgot my costume!" I said.

"It's okay, I didn't bring one either," she answered.

That made me feel a little better, but I still felt stupid at a Halloween costume party without my costume.

We held hands the whole night. We didn't talk much but I really liked being there with her. And she seemed to like it too. We were sitting on the sofa when I felt the vibration of a phone. Mine was in my opposite pocket so I knew it must be hers. She looked down at a text on the screen.

"My mom's here to get me. I have to go," she said.

"I'm leaving soon too, but I had fun," I said quickly.

Kristy smiled. "Me too!" As we stood up she gave me a kiss on the cheek and let go of my hand.

My hand felt numb from being in the same position all night, but I didn't care. I watched as she jumped in her mom's car, waving to me as they drove off.

As they disappeared down the street, dad pulled up. "Get in." His voice was urgent. For a change, I didn't ask why. Dad sped off. "What's going on?" I asked.

"Right after you left Mom got really sick. It came on suddenly. I took her to the hospital and they're keeping her overnight," Dad explained. "She wanted to see you before visiting hours were over though. She's anxious to hear about the party."

I grinned, thinking about Kristy.

"From the looks of that grin it must have gone well—I mean with Kristy and everything," Dad said, smiling.

"Man! Did Mom tell everyone?" I asked, exasperated.

"Pretty much son, pretty much," Dad answered.

They had Mom set up in a room at the end of a long hallway that was plastered with handmade Halloween decorations, obviously made by children. A nurse was taking Mom's blood pressure. She looked okay, nothing like she did a few days ago after her surgery. At least she had the color back in her face. Mom heard us and looked up, giving me a tired smile. Despite her grogginess, she motioned for me to come to her. The nurse smiled at me, retrieved the blood pressure cuff, and left.

"How was your party?" Mom asked, her eyes half-closed.

I couldn't help but smile. "The party was great Mom," I said. "Thanks for making Dad come get me from the shelter. If I would've taken the bus I probably would have missed it."

"So what did you do?" she asked with a mischievous grin.

Like I was going to tell her! I mean, what would I say? Hey, I sat on the sofa holding hands with a beautiful girl all night. No, she didn't need to know, even if it was what she wanted to hear.

"Nothing Mom, we just hung out," I said instead.

"Was Kristy there?" she asked.

"Yeah, she was," I answered. Just the mention of Kristy's name made me smile. Kristy was amazing; I could still feel her soft skin holding my hand. I didn't realize a girl could have such an, effect on me. Mom didn't say anything else—she didn't have to. I'm sure she could tell it went well.

I changed the subject. "So, when do you get to come home?"

She reached out and touched my arm. "In the morning, I feel fine now—just a little tired. The doctor said it was normal, but he wants to keep me overnight just to be sure." She sure seemed groggy. She had an I.V. hanging out of her arm, and I wondered if they had given her something to make her sleepy.

"I'll take James home and then come back," Dad said.

"No, you don't have to. Just come back in the morning," Mom said. "I'm fine. I'll feel better knowing that you're able to get a little sleep. You can't rest in that recliner over there."

"No, don't worry, I want to. I'll feel better being close to you," Dad said.

"Honey, stay home with the boys. Everything is okay here," Mom insisted.

Dad thought for a moment. I knew he would rather sleep at home, but I could tell he was torn.

"Okay, I'll see you in the morning," he said, finally.

Mom smiled at him. He leaned over and kissed her lightly on the lips. They rarely argued, and it was clear that they shared a deep love. I took comfort in that knowledge.

"Let's go, James," Dad said, walking to the door.

Chapter 7

I stepped off the bus in front of Family Safe Haven. Ruth was standing in the doorway again waiting for me. She greeted me with her usual enthusiasm. "Hey James, are you ready for today?"

I wasn't sure if I was ready or not. I hoped I didn't have to clean anything—especially the bathrooms. "Sure Ruth, what did you have in mind?"

"Today you're going to hang out with the kids in the rec room. I hear you're good at video games," she said with a sly wink.

"Yeah, I'm okay," I answered. This didn't sound so bad—if anything it should prove to Dad that I could be responsible and also play video games.

"Great! Follow me." Ruth started down the hallway. I had seen the rec room the first day I'd stumbled into the shelter. She swung the door open and announced, "Kids, this is James. He's going to hang with you today." None of the kids seemed to care, and continued with their various activities.

"Okay James, you take it from here," Ruth said, as she walked back to the door.

I wandered to one of the tables covered with Legos. I had a bunch of Legos when I was younger.

They belonged to Mitchell now. Two boys were playing a video game. I didn't recognize the game they were playing, but most of the games they had here were outdated. Two other boys were playing Ping-Pong. I walked over to their table and introduced myself. One of the boys said, "Hi, I'm Jamal and this is Eric. Are you new here James?"

"No, I just come here to help every once in a while," I answered.

"Where do you live?" Jamal asked.

"I live up by the high school," I said.

"Hmmm. Don't know where that is. I'm from Los Angeles," Jamal said.

"L.A.? How did you get here?" I asked.

"Bus, train, and the back of a pickup truck. I wanted to head East and I'm resourceful," he answered with a smile.

"Wow, that's great." I didn't know what else to say, especially since I had just learned to ride the city bus. In the corner of the room, Chloe sat in her usual spot, just staring at the wall.

"Does she ever play with anyone?" I asked Jamal, motioning at Chloe.

"She don't talk," he said. "None of us ever heard her say anything."

Eric chimed in, "Her mom is nice, but something is wrong with that girl."

"Like what?" I asked, remembering what Ruth had told me about Chloe and her mom before they came to the shelter.

"I'm not sure—no one knows 'cuz she don't tell no one." Jamal and Eric burst into laughter.

I decided to try and talk to Chloe. What would it hurt? Maybe she would talk to me. I walked over and sat down next to her.

"Hi Chloe," I said. She didn't answer, and just continued to stare at the wall.

"Are you excited for Thanksgiving?" I asked.

Still nothing.

"You know Christmas is after that. What do you want for Christmas?" I tried again.

More silence.

"Where's your mom?" I asked.

She just stared blankly at the wall.

She was wearing a pink Dora the Explorer sweatshirt and torn jeans. Her shoes were worn, about a size too big and loose on her feet, unlaced. In fact, she didn't have any shoelaces at all. I looked toward the wall she was staring at, trying to see what was so interesting. There was a picture of three bunnies painted on the wall. I started feeling uncomfortable sitting there in silence, so I stood up and went back over to the Ping-Pong game. Occasionally, I'd glance over to see what Chloe was doing, but she never moved. It made me sad for her. I wondered if she was extremely shy or if she had a condition. I wasn't sure, and for a moment, I also wondered why I cared.

Chapter 8

I stepped off the bus down the street from our house. I'd never realized we had a bus stop so close.

I walked up the street and hopped over the gate into our side yard, surprised to land on freshly planted flowers. The entire flower bed had been planted with winter pansies. I stepped over the flowers, trying to be careful. Mom was standing in the kitchen.

"How many did you trample?" she asked.

"Only a couple. Did you plant all of those flowers?" I asked.

Mom smiled. "I did—and I'm feeling great! I've had a lot of energy today." I could smell something good cooking— there were several pots boiling, a pressure cooker was blowing out steam, and I smelled potatoes. Mom must be making a pot roast with all the fixings.

"Is it for us?" I asked. With Mom you never knew.

"Of course. Dad will be home in a few minutes," she said.

"What can I do to help?" I had promised Dad that I would help around the house, and this seemed like the perfect opportunity. Mom wasn't used to me volunteering to help. She raised her eyebrows.

"Help? Of course you can help. You can start on dessert—pour that whipped cream into a bowl," she said. I attached the blades to the hand mixer, plugged it in, and hit the switch. The blades spun into action, but I didn't have them deep enough in the bowl. Whipped cream slung out and splattered on my shirt. Mom started to laugh and handed me a towel. "Maybe after dinner I can teach you how to do laundry," she said.

I heard the door open as Dad walked into the kitchen. He set his briefcase down on a chair and walked over to Mom. "You look good. How are you feeling?" he asked tenderly.

Mom looked at him with adoring eyes. "I feel great— this new medication is really kicking in."

Dad leaned in and gave her a kiss. As their kiss lingered, I started to fake cough.

"Oh, sorry James," Mom said with a giggle.

Dad looked at me and gave me a wink. "How was the shelter today?"

"It was fine. I hung out with the kids." I didn't want to seem too enthused. I didn't want him to think

I might actually like working at the shelter.

"Good. I'm looking forward to talking with Ruth tomorrow," Dad said.

"Tomorrow? I thought that—"

Dad interrupted me. "You won't have to take the bus tomorrow. I have a meeting with Ruth to discuss Christmas funding. I help her every year with donations."

I had no idea my dad was a philanthropist. I knew he helped out with things, but I had no idea how involved he was. Ruth could use the help.

"Great! I hate the bus," I said.

Mom called, "Dinner's ready!" She took the cream I'd whipped, covered it with plastic, and put it next to the pie in the refrigerator.

Both of my brothers ran in from the game room. Mom was beaming as we all sat down at the table.

Dad said grace, thanking God for Mom and what she was able to accomplish today. Deep inside, I knew days like this were going to be less frequent.

Mom clasped her hands together and said, looking at Dad, "Thanksgiving is only a few weeks away. I want to have the extended family here."

"Are you sure?" Dad answered, surprised.

"Yes, and it'll give me something to look forward to," she said.

"That's fine with me—if you feel up to it," Dad said.

I could see Mom was excited. I didn't know why— hosting Thanksgiving just seemed like a lot of work to me.

"James, you can invite a friend if you want, since none of the cousins are your age," Mom said.

"Thanks Mom, but I'm sure all my friends will want to spend the day with their families," I said.

"That's probably true James, but I wanted you to know it's okay if someone is available." She smiled slyly. Dad started to smile, and looked down at his plate. Suddenly I realized

Mom was telling me I could invite Kristy. My face must have turned red because my brothers started laughing at me.

Normally I'd yell at them, but today I refrained. I didn't want to ruin Mom's dinner. She was clearly happy and I wanted her to stay that way.

Dad volunteered to do the dishes. He recruited me to dry them, I was happy to do it. Mom was getting tired.

"So is Ruth going to tell me you've had a good attitude?" Dad asked as we worked.

"I do what she says," I answered.

"That's not what I'm asking. Do you do what she says with a smile? Or do you act as if it's a chore?" he said.

I had to think about that one. Sometimes I felt like it was a chore, but I was also starting to enjoy the time I spent there. I had never done anything like that before and it kind of made me feel good. "I don't know—I think she likes me," I answered honestly.

"What's not to like?" Dad asked scrubbing a pot.

I hoped Ruth would give him a glowing report. As we finished the dishes, I excused myself.

"Where are you going?" Dad asked.

"I have a ton of homework," I said, drying my palms on my jeans.

"What? Doing homework without being asked? I'm liking this!" Dad said.

I was glad to hear him say that. If I kept this up the car would be in the bag. After all, that's what I was working for.

Chapter 9

I had a brutal day at school, with tests in five of my seven classes. My backpack was full of homework due tomorrow. I didn't really have time for the shelter. In a foul mood, I walked out the front doors and down to the sidewalk. As promised, Dad was waiting for me.

"You ready?" he asked.

"NO! I'm not," I said, more forcefully than I'd meant. "I've had a bad day and my teachers seem to think we're superhuman because we got a ton of homework. I don't think I have time for the shelter today."

"Okay, well—did you commit to going to the shelter today?" Dad asked.

I hung my head. "Yes."

"Okay, then it's up to you, but I know what a responsible person would do," he said.

"Oh, all right." I was stressed!

"Good answer," Dad replied.

Dad had trapped me—I hated it when he gave me the guilt trip, but he must have noticed the stress in my voice.

"Do you really have a lot of homework?" he asked quietly.

"I really do. At least two hours," I said.

"Well, homework is an important responsibility. I'll tell Ruth she can only have you for an hour today. After our meeting I'll take you home," Dad said.

That was a relief. I would have plenty of time to get my homework done, and then maybe I could see if my Australian friend was online.

We pulled up to the shelter and Dad parked the car at the curb. As we entered, Ruth walked out of an office and gave Dad a hug. "Mr. Miller! Thank you so much for coming."

"No problem Ruth. Before we start I must tell you, James needs to leave with me so he only has about an hour," he said.

"Oh? That's too bad," Ruth said, genuinely dismayed.

"I'm sorry Ruth. I just have a lot of homework," I explained.

"No problem, James," Ruth said. "Just go back into the rec room and play with the others. They are looking forward to winning their crown back in ping-pong."

"Ping-Pong?" Dad said surprised.

"Yeah, and he's good," Ruth said. "He whomped the other two boys—but they've been practicing nonstop."

Dad gave me a funny look. "I had no idea," he said perplexed.

I just smiled. I started back to the rec room, but stopped, suddenly getting an idea. "Ruth, do you happen to have a candy bar or something like that?" I asked.

"I do. It's not enough to share with everyone," she said.

"I don't need it for everyone, just one person in particular," I explained.

Ruth smiled. I think she knew what I had in mind. She disappeared into her office and returned with a chocolate bar.

"Perfect! Thanks." I turned and headed for the rec room. As I entered, Jamal and Eric started giving me a hard time. "Did you come back for more?" they taunted.

"For more? If I remember right I beat the socks off both of you," I said.

"Yeah, but tonight we're ready," Eric said. "We'll beat you this time."

"Not tonight guys. I have to leave in a minute so I won't have time for a real match," I said.

"Chicken, bok, bok, bok." They both started flapping their arms like they were wings. I laughed and waved them off, heading over toward the corner to see if Chloe was in her usual chair. Sure enough, there she was, staring at the wall. She had a doll in her hands and was idly running a plastic comb through its hair. Every once in a while she would glance down at the doll. I walked over to her and sat down. "Can I sit here?" I asked quietly. Chloe looked over at me and then glanced away.

"I brought us a treat. Do you like chocolate?" I said.

Chloe looked back at me and nodded her head slightly.

I took the chocolate bar from my pocket, peeled off the wrapper, and broke it in half. I held half of the bar out to her. Cautiously, she reached out and took the candy. She just held it and stared at me. I took the other piece and took a bite. That was all the encouragement she needed, taking a bite out of

the candy as well. Her long, blonde hair was carefully combed today, and she wore the same pink sweatshirt she'd had on the day before. I looked down and noticed she was wearing the same shoes with no shoelaces.

"Chloe, are you excited for Christmas?" I asked.

She didn't say anything, but she at least looked at me and nodded. Well, at least that's progress, I thought to myself.

"What do you want for Christmas?" I asked her.

She turned away from me and looked down at her feet. I figured I had gotten all the communication

I was going to get for one day. "I have to go do my homework now Chloe," I said, standing up. Ruth was standing at the door, smiling at me.

"Did you give that candy bar to Chloe?" Ruth asked as I approached.

I thought I was in for it. I looked down at my feet. "Yes," I said.

"That was really nice," Ruth said. "I'm sure she loved it, but don't get frustrated if she doesn't talk.

No one has been able to reach her."

"I'm not frustrated. She just seems so lonely..." I trailed off. "I don't know, I guess I feel bad for her."

"Don't feel bad. She is well taken care of and her future looks bright. I think her mom is almost ready to move on. They should have an apartment by the first of the year," Ruth said.

"That's great. I mean—that'll be good for both of them," I said, feeling strangely relieved.

"It will be," Ruth agreed. "We try and keep things nice around here, but it's nothing like having your own place."

Just then, Dad walked into the room. "You ready?" he said looking at me.

"Yep, let's go," I answered. I followed Dad out to the car, turning to wave at Ruth as we drove away.

We drove a few miles without saying a word. Dad finally broke the silence. "Ruth gave me a glowing report. She said you are wonderful."

I smiled and shifted in my seat. "So she said I was responsible?"

"Yes she did."

Either Ruth was lying or she really liked me. When we walked in our house, Mom was in the kitchen beaming her usual smile.

"How was it?" she asked.

"Fine Mom, it was fine," I said.

Dad gave Mom a hug and winked at her. "It seems that James is leaving quite the impression at the shelter."

"Yeah, yeah, yeah," I protested.

I walked into the game room—Mitchell was playing a video game. I was about to kick him off when I noticed the game he was playing looked familiar.

"What game is this?" I asked him.

Mitchell didn't take his eyes off the screen. "Bunny Adventures, duh," he replied sarcastically.

The bunnies looked really familiar—and then it dawned on me: Those were the bunnies Chloe stared at on the wall!

"I need to borrow that game," I told Mitchell.

"No way! You can't have it," he answered.

"Not tonight freak, in a few days," I said.

Mitchell seemed satisfied with that. Besides, I had too much homework to think about games right now. Mom had prepared one of my favorites—grilled cheese sandwiches. I grabbed two sandwiches, and headed to my room to hit the books.

Chapter 10

Dad came up about an hour later to check on my progress. I'd grossly underestimated the time it was going to take.

"How's it coming?" he asked.

"Not good, this is taking forever," I groaned.

"Do you have time for a visitor?" he asked?

"Not really," I shot back.

"Okay, I'll send her away," Dad said, turning toward the door.

"Her? Wait, who is it?" I looked up, suddenly interested.

Dad turned and smiled, and I knew it was Kristy.

"Dad, I really want to see her, but I'm never going to finish all of this," I said.

"Tell you what," Dad answered. "Let her know you're buried, and that you can spend half an hour.

I'll help you with this when you're done visiting with Kristy."

I closed my book and hurried downstairs. Kristy was in the kitchen, visiting with Mom. It seemed everyone who met Mom was instantly drawn to her.

Kristy saw me come in and said, "Hi James! I just got my driver's license! Just thought I'd see if you wanted to go for a ride." By this time Dad had walked in. I looked at him and he nodded.

"I can go, but I have to be back in a half an hour. I'm buried in homework," I said.

"Did Mr. Peterson give you a ton?" she asked.

"Yeah," I said with relief. Someone actually understood! "He gave us 30 problems."

"That's what my friend Becky said. I stopped there first and she turned me down," Kristy said.

"Well, let's go!" I didn't want to turn her down. We walked out to her mom's minivan.

"It's not much, but at least she lets me drive it," Kristy explained.

I didn't care what she was driving—I was happy just spending time with her. "It's great," I reassured her.

We hopped in and she slowly backed down the driveway. She reached the road and we started around the block. Kristy was concentrating so much that we weren't even talking. The radio must have been a distraction because she turned it off too. I wasn't sure what to say, or if I should talk at all, but I decided to give it a shot.

"So was the test hard?" I asked.

"The driving test? No, not really. It was pretty easy, but I studied most of last night for it," she said.

"So what was your score?" I asked.

"85%—you only need 75% to pass," she said.

"Wow, that's great! Driving alone must be awesome," I said wistfully.

A small grin crept across her face. "It is, but it's a lot more fun with someone in the car," she said, flirting.

I felt my stomach flutter. We drove in silence a little longer. The time was flying by! We suddenly realized we'd been driving 25 minutes, and it would take another 10 minutes to get back to my house.

I didn't want this drive to end, but I'd made a deal with Dad. A responsible person would uphold his side of the bargain.

"As much as I hate to say it, we'd better head back to my house," I said reluctantly.

"Oh, bummer!" Kristy smiled, turned around, and headed back. When she got to the gate I gave her the key code. She pushed the buttons and the gate slowly opened. As she pulled up to our house, I thought of what Mom had said about inviting someone over for Thanksgiving—this would be the perfect opportunity.

"My mom said I could invite someone over for Thanksgiving. Do you want to come over?" I said.

"I mean, I understand if you have family stuff, but I would love it if you—"

"Oh James, I can't," Kristy said, obviously disappointed, "We go to my Grandma's every year.

Sorry…" Her voice trailed off. I understood. I would also be spending the holiday with my Grandma.

"Well, I'd better get in. It feels like I'm never going to finish all this homework," I said.

"Yeah, of course," Kristy said. "Thanks for going with me."

"Thanks for the offer! Come by anytime," I said, reaching for the door. I watched as she slowly backed down the drive.

As I went back into the house, Mom and Dad were staring at me as if I had just come back from the moon. "So how was it?" Mom asked excitedly.

"We drove around the block a few times, not a big deal," I said.

Nate decided to give me a hard time, "James loves Kristy, James loves Kristy," he chanted. I just stood there and listened to him. If Dad weren't here I probably would have punched Nate. Hard. But I didn't want to upset Dad. "Nate!" Dad spoke up just then. "Knock it off." I returned to my room and to my books, but even with Dad's help I found it extremely hard to concentrate.

Chapter 11

I opened my backpack for the 100th time to make sure the Bunny Adventures game was there. I was hoping Chloe would like it. As the bus pulled up to the stop I saw Ruth standing in the doorway waiting for me.

"James!" she said enthusiastically.

"Hi Ruth, what do you have in mind for today?"

"I really only have one job today—unless you want to help serve dinner?" she asked.

"Well, what's the job?" I wanted to know what the job was before I committed to dinner.

"I need the pantry organized. We just took in a large food donation that needs to be sorted and put away. It shouldn't take long, so you'll have plenty of time for Ping-Pong later," Ruth said.

"Sounds good to me. Just show me what to do," I said, as I followed Ruth to a large pantry. Several pallets of food were stacked in the middle of the room. The shelves were almost bare, but the pallets of food would take care of that.

"Okay, open the boxes and put all the cans on that side of the wall," she said pointing to the left.

"And the boxes on this side."

"Seems easy enough," I said, taking off my sweatshirt.

"It's not hard—shouldn't take you more than an hour or so." Ruth smiled and walked out of the pantry while I got busy unloading boxes. I wanted to hurry to the rec room to show Chloe what I'd brought. Soon I had all the food sorted and stacked, and the boxes flattened and moved to the recycling bin. I found Ruth in the kitchen giving some last minute directions before starting dinner.

"So, how did it go?" she asked.

"Well it's done, so it went just fine," I told Ruth with a wink.

"Great! You earned some time in the rec room. All of the kids have had their dinner, so just head on back," she said.

I didn't hesitate. I really wanted to find Chloe. As I entered the rec room, Jamal was sitting in a chair, tapping a Ping-Pong paddle on the table. I looked around, but didn't see Eric anywhere.

"Where's Eric?" I asked.

"Gone," Jamal answered glumly.

"Gone where?"

"His family got an apartment. He isn't here anymore," he said.

"When did this happen?" I asked.

"Yesterday," Jamal replied quietly, obviously missing his friend.

"So you don't have anyone to play with?" I asked.

"Nope—not unless you want to lose," he said.

I looked around the room for Chloe; she was nowhere to be seen. A quick game of Ping-Pong would be fun while I waited for Chloe.

"You're on! Except for the losing part," I said.

We played three games. I won two games—Jamal one. He was a little upset, but I had quite the knack for Ping-Pong. I was doing my victory dance when I saw Chloe walk into the room and sit down in her usual spot in the corner.

"That's it for me Jamal," I said, laying my paddle on the table.

As I walked over to Chloe, Jamal taunted me to play again, but I ignored him. I sat down next to Chloe, opened up my backpack, and fumbled through it until I found the bunny game.

"Do you know this game?" I held the game up for Chloe to see.

She looked at the cover and nodded, pointing at the bunnies on the wall.

"That's right, they're the same thing," I said, encouraged.

Chloe held the game box and looked at the wall.

"Chloe, this is a game. We can play it on the TV," I said. She didn't respond. I held out my hand.

She turned then, and stared at my hand for a minute.

"Do you want to play the game?" I asked.

She finally nodded and took my hand. I led her to the game console, inserted the disk, and the game menu appeared on the screen. I gave her a crash course on how the game worked. She started pressing buttons, which made the bunnies move on the screen. She seemed to love it—I thought I even heard her laugh softly a few times. An hour flew by, and before I knew it, I had to go.

"Chloe I have to go now. That game belongs to my brother. Do you think I should take it home to him?" I asked.

She nodded yes. I shut off the machine and put the game back into its case. Chloe stood up and walked back to her corner. Ruth was waiting for me as I walked back towards the exit with a huge smile.

"Don't be disappointed," Ruth told me.

"I know—she never talks, but she came a long way today," I said.

"I agree James, but unfortunately she still has a long way to go. I'm not sure if Chloe will be here long enough for us to hear her talk," Ruth cautioned.

"Really? Watch this." I turned around and hollered, "Chloe!" She turned and looked in my direction. I waved at her. She looked at me, smiled, and waved back.

"Well, I'll be. You may actually get her talking," Ruth said, obviously surprised.

"Who knows? But it's sure fun trying," I said.

"Go catch your bus—you don't want to miss it," she replied. I walked out just as the bus pulled up.

I hopped on, paid the fee, and sat down. I'd had a good time today. I was excited to come back and see Chloe again.

Chapter 12

Because of teacher prep days, we had two days off before Thanksgiving. On Tuesday, I woke up early to help Mom rake leaves; our lawn was completely covered. She had brought several large plastic bags from the garage. She held a rake out toward me, and said, "Rake the leaves into piles—

I'll scoop them up."

As we raked I noticed that our lawn, which at first had looked yellow, was actually a vibrant green.

"James look—you're painting the lawn green!" Mom joked. I could always count on Mom to appreciate the little things in life.

Before I knew it, we had filled over a dozen bags. I dragged each one out to the curb, piling them up as best I could.

"Wow! I had no idea we would use so many," Mom said proudly. "Well believe it, 'cause here they are," I said. Mom's face lit up with a smile and suddenly I realized that it was possible that

Mom's smile was going to be taken from us forever. I felt a wave of sadness, but immediately chased the thought away.

"Thanks for your help James. I appreciate it." Mom put her arm around me and gave me a squeeze.

I returned the hug. "So what are your plans for the rest of your day off school?"

I looked at my watch and realized that I had to get to the bus stop. "I told Ruth I would help her at the shelter today," I said.

"You better hurry, I don't want you to miss the bus." Mom was right—there was no time to spare. I put the rake back in the garage and headed down the street, barely reaching the bus stop in time. Once on the bus and alone with my thoughts, I couldn't help but think, My mom is so cool!

The weather had turned cold and the shelter was packed. I had an idea about how to maybe get through to Chloe, but I had to run it past Ruth first. Ruth was in the back, talking to a bunch of people.

It looked like she was guiding a tour, but as I got closer I could hear her telling everyone the winter rules for the shelter. She must have finished, because the crowd started to disperse.

"James!" Ruth always seemed so excited to see me.

"Before you give me an assignment, I want to bounce an idea off you," I said.

"Okay, shoot," Ruth answered.

"I want to paint with Chloe today. Does the shelter have any paint?" Ruth thought about it for a moment. "We've got paint, but I'm not so sure she'll want to."

"I'm not sure either, but my eight-year-old brother loves to paint. I think it's worth a try," I said.

"Okay, do it. There's a closet in the rec room. The paints are on the top shelf," she said.

"Thanks Ruth!" I hurried to the rec room. Chloe was in her usual spot. I walked over and sat down.

"Hi Chloe," I said. She looked at me—a little friendlier today, but still silent.

"Do you want to paint today?" I asked. She just stared at me as if she didn't understand what I was

trying to say.

"You know, paint on paper. Paint pictures," I persisted.

Chloe looked at me and nodded. I jumped up and retrieved the paints from the top shelf of the closet. I spread them out on the table along with some paper. I handed her a brush. She just stared at it in her hand. I picked up a brush and dipped it in the paint. I started to paint a car. Chloe caught on quickly and she started to paint on the paper. She started to paint what looked like a turkey.

"Is that a turkey?" I asked.

She smiled and nodded.

"Do you like turkey?"

She nodded again. Another idea struck me—I had to find Ruth. I told Chloe to stay put and ran to find Ruth in the kitchen.

"Can Chloe come to my house for Thanksgiving? Mom said I could invite a friend. I want to invite

Chloe," I said.

"It's not up to me—it's up to her mom," Ruth said.

"Her mom can come too," I answered.

"Well you're in luck." Ruth pointed down the hall toward the rec room. Chloe's mom had come in to see her painting. I hurried back down the hall and sat at the table next to Chloe.

"Are you helping her with this?" Charlotte asked, surprised.

"Yeah, I asked her if she wanted to paint. I'm James," I said, offering my hand. She took my hand and replied, "Nice to meet you James. I'm Charlotte." She continued quietly, "Chloe hasn't done anything like this in a long time."

That seemed really sad to me. "Can I ask you a question?" I suddenly felt nervous and I wasn't sure why.

"Sure, go ahead," Charlotte said.

"Can Chloe come to my house for Thanksgiving? I can invite a friend and I want her to come. Mom makes a great meal," I said.

"Oh, I don't know," Charlotte replied quickly. She seemed taken aback. "I really don't know you or your parents."

"You can come too," I said. I was sure Mom wouldn't mind. "There's always plenty and we'd be happy to have you."

Charlotte thought about that for a moment. "I'm not sure if I'd feel comfortable," she said finally.

"Oh, come on, it'll be great. You'll love my mom."

"I'll think about it," she finally agreed. I didn't want her to think about it—I just wanted her to say yes. But I also didn't want to be too aggressive, so I backed off.

Ruth had come into the room and heard part of our exchange. She pulled Charlotte aside and they spoke for about five minutes. Ruth talked quietly, but I could hear her telling Charlotte how wonderful my family was and that Chloe would be completely safe; she even said that it would be a great

74

experience for her. Meanwhile, I resumed my painting with Chloe. Ruth left the room as Charlotte approached me.

"Based on what Ruth just told me, I'll let Chloe go. But I want your dad to pick her up so I can meet him," Charlotte said.

She smiled and walked away. I looked down at Chloe. "Do you want to come eat turkey at my house on Thanksgiving?" I asked.

She looked up at me, concerned. "If you don't like it we'll bring you right back," I said quickly.

Chloe's face lit up. She nodded yes.

I was thrilled, but now I had to explain to Mom and Dad that I had invited a homeless girl to Thanksgiving dinner.

Chapter 13

I spent the bus ride home thinking about what I was going to say to Mom. I didn't know why I was so worried. Mom wouldn't mind—at least I didn't think she would.

I walked in the side door next to the garage. Mom was in the kitchen. She saw me and smiled.

"How was the shelter?"

"It was good." I wasn't sure if this was a good time to tell her, but I decided the sooner the better.

"You know how you told me I could have a friend over for Thanksgiving?"

A grin crept across Mom's face. "Yes?" She said.

"Well, I invited a friend."

"You invited Kristy, right?" Mom said.

"Well, no, not exactly—I mean I did, but she's going to her grandparents," I said.

"So who did you invite?" she asked cautiously.

"Chloe!" I said, as if she knew who Chloe was.

"And who, may I ask, is Chloe?" Mom answered.

"She's a girl I met at the shelter," I said quickly.

"Oh, she volunteers?"

"Not exactly. She's a guest," I said.

Mom looked concerned. "I'm not sure I like the idea of you going out with girls that live in the shelter—not that they don't deserve… But…it's just that—" Mom was stammering so I decided some reassurance might help calm her. "Mom, Chloe is nine," I explained.

"Nine?"

"Yep. And she doesn't talk," I added.

"She doesn't talk?"

"She's great Mom, and she's really a cute little girl. She's had a pretty rough life, but her mother is almost back on her feet, and they will be moving out of the shelter soon. I don't think Chloe has ever had a real Thanksgiving dinner," I said.

Mom smiled. "Of course she can come! Good for you to think to invite her. This is going to be great! What about her mother? Will she come too?"

"I invited her, but she didn't want to impose. I told her it would be fine, but she said no. She wants to meet Dad when we pick up Chloe, though."

"Well, we're eating around two, so tell her you and Dad will pick her up around 1:30," Mom said.

"Perfect! I'll call Ruth and let her know." I gave Mom a hug and went to get my phone. I was excited. I don't know why, but there was something inside me that told me this was just the right thing to do. Now I couldn't wait until Thursday!

"Don't forget—you said you would help me tomorrow," Mom reminded me.

"Okay Mom, I remember." With all the excitement I had actually forgotten, but I didn't mind helping anymore. And it would mean one more "check" on the responsibility list. I could almost smell the interior of my new car.

Chapter 14

I woke up the day before Thanksgiving to find Mom in the kitchen making waffles. I love Mom's waffles.

"Good morning, sweetheart," she said with a smile.

"Morning, Mom. The waffles sure smell good," I answered.

"I hope so. We're ready to eat. Go get your brothers."

I turned and yelled up the stairs, "Waffles!"

"I could have done that James!" Mom exclaimed.

Moments later, I heard pounding feet on the stairs and looked over to see Nate and Mitchell standing in the kitchen.

"Well it worked didn't it?" I replied. She shot me a stern look and turned to pull a waffle from the iron. She cut the waffle in half and gave half to Nate and the other half to Mitchell.

"You'll have to wait," she said pointing her spatula at me. I sat on a bar stool at the counter with an empty plate and a growling stomach. Dad walked into the kitchen a few moments later, wandered toward Mom and gave her a big hug and one of those lingering kisses that made us all turn our heads away.

"Good morning," she said, a little flirty. He just smiled. I rolled my eyes.

The waffle iron started to beep. Mom pulled out the waffle, put it on a plate, and handed it to Dad.

"Hey!" I protested.

"You're going to have to wait," Mom said.

"What did James do?" Dad asked.

"I asked him to go get his brothers and instead he became his own personal intercom and yelled for them up the stairs," she said.

"Well, did it work?" Dad asked?

Mom playfully slapped Dad on the shoulder while Dad and I laughed. The waffle iron beeped again. Mom placed the warm waffle on my plate. I buttered it, and topped it off with a shot of whipped cream.

"James, I know what I want you to do today," Mom said.

"Name it, Mom," I answered through a mouthful of waffle.

"I want you go down and get the Christmas tree and set it up by the stairs," she said.

"Honey, it's Thanksgiving. Can't we get that out of the way first?" Dad asked. The look Mom gave

Dad told him to back off. "Do what she asks then James," Dad reluctantly told me.

Stuffed with three waffles, I climbed down the stairs to the basement. The Christmas decorations were in a cold storage room under the porch. I dug around and finally found the Christmas tree. At 15 feet tall, it was so large it was stored in three boxes. I dragged the boxes to where Mom wanted the tree set up, in the front foyer next to the winding staircase. I enlisted Nate to help hold the base of the tree while I assembled the pieces on top. I heard Mom asking Mitchell to come in and help us.

Hanging the ornaments was the best part. Every year Mom would let us hang all the ornaments by ourselves. We each had our own ornaments that we were in charge of placing on the tree—they were the ones we had picked out each year at the mall a few weeks before Christmas. She would always tell us what a great job we did and how beautiful the tree was. We always thought it was strange when we awoke the next morning to find all of the ornaments rearranged. Mom would never admit she'd changed it, but in her defense, it always looked much better. We took our time and hung every last one. When we were done we called Mom in. "Boys, this looks better than ever! I might not even have to rearrange anything this year," she said.

"Ah-ha! I knew it! Every year you rearrange the tree!" I was practically shouting.

Mom acted shocked. "Well no, not usually—okay maybe a little." Mom smiled at us. She reached out and ruffled Mitchell's hair before walking back into the kitchen.

"Here's the real test," I said flipping the light switch. The tree lit up and the ornaments sparkled from the light of the bulbs. I had to agree—the tree looked pretty impressive. Mom walked back into the foyer and shook her head. I saw a tear begin in the corner of her eye. "I love it," she said softly.

"You guys really did a good job! Oh and there's one more thing." She left, and returned a few minutes later holding three small boxes. She handed one to each of us and smiled. "Open them!"

We eagerly opened our gifts to find angels inside. Mom smiled. "I want you to hang these on the tree every year from now on. Make it a tradition," she said.

"You'll have to be sure to remind us next year," I told Mom. She gave me a hug. "You bet James,

I'll be sure to remind you." She quickly turned and walked from the room brushing tears away from her eyes. I thought I should go after her to see if she was okay, but I didn't. Instead I stared up at the tree. It was truly magnificent and I knew one thing—Chloe was going to love it.

Chapter 15

I awoke Thanksgiving morning to the sound of pots and pans crashing together. I jumped out of bed and ran downstairs to see what was going on. Mom was on a step stool and Dad was steadying her as she reached for the pots on the top shelf in the pantry. Dishes were scattered all over the counter. It was time to start the cooking.

"It's not too late to have it catered," Dad said. "In fact—"

"I want to do the cooking, and it is too late to cater." Mom was determined to make a feast.

Grandma usually brought a few dishes and Aunt Kelly usually brought the pies, but Mom did the rest, and it was always fantastic.

When it was finally time to go get Chloe, Mom was still cooking up a storm. Dad felt guilty leaving her, but we had to go. Dad quickly backed down the drive and headed for the shelter. The streets were empty so we made good time. As we pulled up to the curb, as usual, Ruth was waiting by the door. She waved at us as Dad and I got out of the car.

"Happy Thanksgiving!" Ruth called as we approached.

"Happy Thanksgiving Ruth," Dad and I said together. Chloe and Charlotte were waiting inside for us. They smiled as we approached.

Dad held out his hand to Charlotte. "Hi, my name is Spencer Miller." Charlotte shook his hand.

"I'm Charlotte, and this is my daughter Chloe," she said pointing in Chloe's direction. Dad knelt down on one knee and said, "Hi Chloe." Chloe smiled, but as usual she didn't say anything.

I reached out to Chloe, "Are you ready to go?" She nodded and took my hand. As we filed out the door toward Dad's car, Dad unlocked the door and I helped Chloe into the back seat. As I put the seat belt on her, Charlotte poked her head into the car. "Now you be good, okay?" Chloe smiled and nodded at her. Charlotte gave her a kiss on her forehead and shut the car door.

"We'll take good care of her," Dad said. Ruth put her arm around Charlotte. "We know—now you go and have fun!" she said.

"Charlotte, you're more than welcome to come," Dad offered.

Charlotte smiled. "I know, and thank you, but I'll stay here. I want to help Ruth anyway, maybe start a new tradition."

Dad smiled. "We'll be back by nine if that's okay?"

"That's fine, we'll see you then," Charlotte said.

Dad started the car and we drove away. I couldn't wait for Chloe to see the tree.

Dad pulled up the driveway and parked in the garage. I helped Chloe out of the car. I walked her around the front of the house so she would see the tree first. Her eyes opened wide, twinkling with amazement. She walked to the base of the tree and looked up. The glow of the lights didn't compare to the glow on Chloe's face when Mom walked in the room.

"This must be Chloe," she said warmly. "Come into the kitchen, we're almost ready." Chloe just looked at Mom and smiled.

I motioned for Chloe to follow me into the kitchen to meet my Grandparents and Aunt Kelly.

"Everyone," I announced, "this is Chloe." Everyone chimed back, "Hi Chloe!" in unison. I was worried she might be a little overwhelmed since she was so shy, but she was still smiling—I figured she was doing okay.

The table was set with the turkey in the center. We all took our places—Mom had a special place set for Chloe next to me. Chloe climbed onto her chair and sat with her hands in her lap. Mom was the last to sit down, and she looked over at Dad.

"I'm going to say a prayer," he started. "We are thankful this day for our many blessings. We are thankful for family and friends who have joined with us to eat this beautiful meal. We are thankful for..." Dad stopped talking for a moment. I looked up and noticed he was crying. He composed himself and went on. "We are so thankful for Jan and all the hard work she put into this meal. Bless her, be with her, I pray...Amen."

We all looked up. I wasn't quite sure why Dad was so emotional, but both of my Grandparents had tears in their eyes as well. I glanced at Chloe and wondered how she was taking all of this. She looked concerned.

Mom decided it was time to cheer everybody up. "Dig in everyone, and pass me the potatoes," she said.

As the food was passed around the table, I helped Chloe load up her plate. She was capable of doing it herself, but she was still a little timid. She was used to the shelter where you couldn't eat as much as you wanted, and I wanted to make sure she got enough to eat. There was a lot of food on the table. Chloe just kept looking around, taking it all in.

Everything tasted so good. Mom was getting compliments from everyone. She kept looking at Dad and smiling. It was hard to believe she was sick, but I knew she still was. I'd overheard them talking about her condition many times. I wanted to ignore it and thought it might go away if I did. I just wanted her to get better. For a brief moment, I wondered if this could be her last Thanksgiving. I chased the thought away immediately. She was going to be okay. At least that's what I kept telling myself.

Everyone pitched in to help with the cleanup. Dad told Mom to sit down and take a break, but she wouldn't hear of it. She wanted to be in the middle of everything, surrounded by the people she loved so much.

After dinner, Mom always brought out games for everyone to play. It was a Thanksgiving tradition at our house. Nate started going through the boxes of games to see if anything looked interesting.

Chloe sat in the chair next to Mom staring at the pile with wide eyes. Mom looked at Chloe and smiled.

"So Chloe, tell me what you want for Christmas," Mom said.

I shot Mom a look to remind her Chloe doesn't talk, but Chloe then shocked us all.

"Shoelaces," Chloe said in a small voice. She caught everyone off guard—especially me! The room fell silent for what seemed like minutes. I couldn't believe what I'd just heard.

"What? What did you say?" I finally asked, surprised.

"I want shoelaces for Christmas," Chloe repeated, a little louder this time.

Mom looked at Chloe's shoes and noticed they were a size too big, and the shoelaces were missing.

"How about new shoes?" Mom asked.

"I don't need shoes," Chloe said smiling. "I need shoelaces so my shoes will stay on my feet." I wished Charlotte and Ruth were here to hear this! Chloe hadn't spoken a word in a very long time.

"Okay," Mom surrendered. "You need shoelaces but what else do you want? Maybe a doll?"

"I want shoelaces. I already have a doll," Chloe said softly.

"But don't you—" Mom started, but Dad cut her off.

"It's okay if she just wants shoelaces," Dad said.

Mom gave up, but had tears in her eyes. We all did. I had a whole list of things I wanted for Christmas, including a car, and I would most likely get everything on my list.

Chloe wanted one thing—shoelaces to hold her shoes on her feet. And I didn't know if she would even get that. She had probably never had a big Christmas like I was used to. It made me feel bad for her and I wanted to do something to help. It was the first time in my life that I began to think about giving for Christmas, rather than getting.

We played games until Dad announced at 8:30 that it was time to take Chloe back to the shelter.

Mom handed her a sack with some rolls inside. "Give these to your mom, okay?"

Chloe nodded at Mom and then gave her a big hug—something I don't think Mom was expecting, but she welcomed. We walked to the car, and I again buckled Chloe into the back seat. As we drove back to the shelter I thought about how special the day had been. Mom's day had been good, and it was so exciting to hear Chloe finally talk! Looking at her, it was obvious she had enjoyed herself as well. I was happy with my decision to invite her. Ruth was waiting for us on the sidewalk, with her customary smile.

"Hey!" she said as she opened the back door. "Did you have a good time Chloe?"

Chloe hesitated, but then said quietly, "Yes." Ruth stopped in her tracks. She slowly turned to look at me, then over to Dad. He just shrugged his shoulders. I could tell Ruth was stunned.

"Chloe, was that you?" Ruth asked, fighting back tears.

"Yes." Chloe answered, a little more confidently this time.

"Your mom is going to be so happy!" Ruth said.

Chloe just nodded and smiled.

Ruth disappeared into the shelter and we followed her inside. Ruth was holding a phone to her ear and dialing a number.

"Charlotte, Chloe is back," Ruth said, pure excitement in her voice. "Yes, you can meet her down here. I'll be here waiting."

Ruth hung up the phone. "Your mom is going to be so shocked to hear your voice," she said with her hands on her hips.

A few moments later Charlotte walked into the room. She smiled when she saw Chloe, and held her arms open as Chloe ran to her. Charlotte scooped her up and held her tight.

"Did you have fun Chloe?" Charlotte asked.

"They had the biggest Christmas tree!" Chloe said.

"They did?—" suddenly Charlotte stopped talking. Stunned, she put her hand over her mouth and turned her head to look at her daughter. "Wait, Chloe, did you say something?"

"I said they had a big Christmas tree!"

Charlotte burst into tears and hugged Chloe tightly. Finally she said, "She's talking! When did this start?"

"My mom asked her what she wanted for Christmas and she answered," I explained.

"Oh my goodness, and I wasn't there. This is so amazing! Thank you! Thank you so much James!"

Charlotte walked over and gave me a hug. She was trembling from excitement. "Thank you," she said

through her tears. "She hasn't said a word in so long. I don't know how—"

"It wasn't me. It was my mom. Chloe really took to her." I wanted to take the credit, but it wasn't me Chloe had answered.

"Well then, please thank your mom for me." Charlotte said earnestly.

"I will," I said.

Chloe walked into the other room, giving Charlotte the opportunity to ask, "What did she say she wanted for Christmas?"

"She said she wanted shoelaces," I said.

Charlotte's eyes welled up with tears that spilled onto her cheeks. She didn't say anything, just stood there with her hand to her mouth crying.

"Are you okay?" Dad asked putting an arm around her.

"I'm fine, it's just..." She buried her face in her hands and openly wept. Ruth put her arm around

Charlotte too, and started patting her back. "When we were on the streets my backpack broke. I had to use her shoelaces as rope to hold the pack together. They were ruined and I haven't bothered to get her another pair. I didn't realize she noticed." She was talking in between sobs. "What kind of a mother can't even provide shoelaces for her daughter?"

"Don't sell yourself short," Dad said, "You're doing your best now to give her the kind of life she deserves. You have no idea the impact you have on your daughter—and believe me it extends way beyond having shoelaces. We would love to have her again—maybe in a week or so?"

"That would be great. It's obvious she enjoyed herself." Charlotte seemed grateful.

Charlotte seemed to take some comfort in what Dad said. "Thanks again for all you did for her today," Charlotte said as she turned away to go find Chloe.

"It was our pleasure," Dad said. "I think we enjoyed it as much as Chloe did, and we were happy to have her."

On the way back home I reflected on the day's events. I must have been more tired than I thought because the sound of the tires rolling over the driveway woke me up. I'd slept most of the way home.

As I dragged myself into the house I was thinking of Chloe and her Christmas wish. Shoelaces, I thought to myself as I looked around the room. We were blessed with so many things, and Chloe had nothing—but she didn't even complain about it. Mom was right when she told me I was spoiled.

Chloe made me want to be better. Something had started to change inside me. I thought about how much she loved her mom, even after all that had happened in her life. Then I thought about the way I acted with my brothers and my parents. What if I woke up one day and they were gone? What if I never had the chance to make up for the way I treated them? I needed to be better.

Mom was sitting at the kitchen table waiting for us. "You did a good thing today," she said with pride.

"Very responsible, son," Dad chimed in.

"I didn't invite her over to be responsible—I invited her because I thought she would like it," I said.

"Well it worked—I think she was very happy. And she spoke, that had to be a big surprise to her mother," Mom said.

"She cried!" I said.

Dad walked up and put his arm around my shoulders. "I'm proud of you. You acted on instinct. You weren't trying to impress anyone, you just did the right thing."

90

For once I wasn't thinking of the car, and it felt pretty good to have Dad say he was proud of me.

"I want to have her over again," Mom said.

"I'm sure she would love it," I said. "When did you have in mind?"

"I want to make my Christmas cookies next week. I thought it would be fun for her to come over and help," Mom said. Every year Mom made Christmas cookies for friends and our family—the kitchen usually turned into a disaster zone. I could taste them already.

"I'll ask Charlotte, but I'm sure she won't mind," I said.

Dad looked concerned again. "Do you think you're up to it this year, Jan?"

"If I was able to take on Thanksgiving, I'm sure I can handle cookies. Besides, Grandma said she would help out, and it keeps my mind occupied," Mom relied.

Dad seemed satisfied and headed out to the family room while Mom pulled out her recipe book and started making a list of ingredients she would need.

"What day should I tell her?" I asked.

"Plan on next Saturday, I want to do it on a weekend so school doesn't get in the way," Mom said, working on her list. I couldn't wait to go back to the shelter on Monday to talk to Charlotte.

Chapter 16

Cookie day came fast. I had spent three days after school at the shelter this past week. Chloe was talking up a storm. Charlotte thanked me every time I walked in the door, and she was more than happy to let Chloe come to our house for cookie day. My stock with Ruth had gone way up as well.

The December air was extra cold today as Dad and I pulled up in front of the shelter—so cold that

I tried to avoid taking deep breaths because it burned my lungs. Ruth and Chloe were waiting for us inside the shelter. Chloe was wearing her usual pink sweatshirt.

"Chloe, do you have a coat?" Dad asked. She shook her head. Ruth smiled and pulled a coat out of a closet, and helped Chloe into it. "You can wear this one for today."

"Thanks, Ruth," Chloe said. I enjoyed hearing Chloe's voice; we'd both come a long way since our first meeting.

I helped Chloe into the car and we headed for home. We could smell the cookies as soon as we walked inside. Mom rushed over and gave Chloe a hug. "Welcome back Chloe, are you ready to help frost cookies?"

"What do I do?" Chloe asked.

Mom got her situated at the counter and handed her a plastic knife. She had made three different colors of frosting, and there were several different shapes of sugar cookies spread out on the counter.

Mom picked up a snowman shaped cookie.

"All you do is scoop some frosting on the knife and spread it out on the cookie." Mom showed her how to do one, and then handed her the frosting and a plastic knife.

Chloe caught on quickly and started frosting cookies. Mom had also put out some candy to use for decorations. Chloe looked at the candy with wide eyes; Mom knew what she wanted.

"You can have some candy, but not too much—we're ordering pizza for lunch," Mom said with a smile.

Chloe smiled back and put a jawbreaker in her mouth. I just sat and watched. Grandma was washing dishes, and Mom and Chloe seemed to have the decorating under control. About an hour later

Mom ordered the pizza. Dad said he'd pick it up, so I decided to go with him. The pizzeria was only a few blocks away. As we walked into the garage Dad shocked me. He handed me the keys to the car.

"You're driving," he announced.

I had driven his car, but only in a parking lot. I was so excited! I looked at him to make sure he wasn't kidding, but he was already climbing into the passenger seat. I got in and put the keys in the ignition. I was a little worried about backing out of the garage, but I managed it just fine.

Dad only gave me a few suggestions on the way to the pizzeria. I obediently replied, "Right, Dad."

I smiled—no amount of criticism could ruin this drive for me. I didn't have any problems getting there. Dad went in and returned with three giant pizzas.

"Your mother seems to think we're feeding an army," he said.

"Three pizzas? Is anyone else coming over?" I asked.

"Not that I'm aware of, but you never know with your mom," Dad replied. I managed to drive us safely back home. As we carried the pizzas into the kitchen, I was surprised to see Kristy sitting next to Chloe, frosting cookies. Kristy looked up at me and smiled.

"Hi James!" she said.

Mom smiled at me. "I thought it would be fun for Kristy to meet Chloe."

I didn't like it when Mom did things like this, but I quickly forgave her—I was just glad to see Kristy.

Kristy boldly gave me a hug. I must have blushed because Mom and Dad started laughing. She whispered in my ear, "Your mom told me the about the amazing things you're doing at the shelter. I think it's really sweet!" The warmth of her breath made my skin tingle. Kristy walked back to her spot by Chloe.

Mom put pizza on plates for everyone. Chloe looked at the pizza like she'd never seen one before.

"I don't get pizza very often," she said.

"Well eat up, there's plenty." Mom announced. Nate and Mitchell came running in from the game room to grab a slice. Mom handed Chloe plate of pizza. Chloe was so excited she clapped her hands together.

"I wish my mom could be here for pizza," she said. Chloe sat down next to my mom and started talking. I thought I was safe to sit next to Kristy. I didn't want Chloe to think I was paying more attention to Kristy, but Chloe seemed to be having the time of her life just talking with Mom. I grabbed a slice of pizza and sat down. Kristy looked at me and slid a little closer.

She spoke so only I could hear her. "Chloe is awesome. What's her mom like?" I thought for a moment and in between bites I answered, "She's amazing. They've had to stay at the shelter for a while now, but her mom has been working hard to get out. They've found an apartment, so they will be moving soon."

"Where is the apartment?" Kristy asked.

"I don't know, I hadn't thought to ask," I said.

"I just wonder if she is staying here or if she is moving to another town?" Kristy commented.

I suddenly had a pit in my stomach. What if they were moving to another town? I had never thought about that possibility. Chloe was starting to feel like part of the family, and I knew if she left I would miss her even though I hadn't known her long.

After everyone finished eating, Mom let Chloe put some cookies on a plate for her and her Mom.

Chloe's face lit up—it was obvious she wanted to show Charlotte her frosted creations. It was time for us to take her back to the shelter, so Mom helped Chloe into her borrowed coat. I asked Kristy if she wanted to go with us, but she volunteered to stay and help Mom and Grandma with the cleanup.

Just as Dad and I started walking Chloe to the garage, Mom ran up to Chloe. "I need a big hug, little one." Chloe wrapped her arms around Mom's neck and gave her a squeeze. Mom pulled back and said, "Let me see the inside of that coat." She pulled out the tag on the coat Chloe was wearing. Dad looked over at me and winked. I knew Mom had an ulterior motive. She was going to buy Chloe a coat. I was finally beginning to see how often Mom did nice things like that.

Chloe said goodbye and turned to walk out the door but stopped suddenly in the foyer, staring at the wall. I looked over to see what had caught her eye. It was a picture of Jesus that Mom had hung by the front door. Chloe just stared at it. Mom had told us many times the picture was to remind us of who we are, and she wanted that to be the last thought we had as we left the house. No one said a word as we waited for Chloe.

After a few seconds she looked at me. "Who is that man in the picture?" I looked at Mom and then over to Dad. They both nodded their heads as if to say, tell her.

"That's Jesus, Chloe. Do you know who Jesus is?" I asked.

"Ruth told me, but the picture of Jesus at the shelter looks nothing like this," she said.

"What does the picture at the shelter look like?" I asked.

"Jesus is hanging on a cross—he looks hurt," Chloe said.

In the picture by our door, Jesus was pictured in a crimson robe. "So what do you think of this picture?" Mom asked.

No one was prepared for what Chloe said next. "That's the man who sat next to me under the bridge in the rain," she answered. Mom finally broke our shocked silence.

"Can you tell us about it?" she asked.

Chloe nodded her head. "It was dark and cold and raining. We were trying to find shelter, but there was nothing around. I followed Mom under a bridge to stay dry. Mom had to leave and told me to stay there. I didn't know where she was going and I was scared. I saw two men heading toward me in the shadows. They looked real mean. As they got closer, a hand covered my hand. I looked next to me and that man was sitting beside me." Chloe pointed at the picture. "He told me he made me invisible.

I watched as the two scary men walked up, but they looked around and then headed away. When that man left he told me, 'You will find somewhere safe tonight, don't be scared.' Then he left. As soon as he left, Mom came back and told me she found somewhere for us. We walked up to the road and Ruth was standing there next to a car. We got in and she took us to the shelter."

By this time everyone else had come in to see what was going on, because we were all crying now.

Once again, Chloe had touched us all in a way that only she could. She was truly a special little girl.

Dad finally said, "Well, we should get you back home Chloe." Mom knelt down and opened her arms wide. Chloe walked over and allowed Mom to gather her up in a hug. "Thank you so much for telling us that story. You just made my day," Mom said still teary. She held Chloe close for a moment.

Watching Mom with Chloe made me feel good. Mom looked truly happy and I was glad. As she finally let Chloe go, Dad and I took Chloe back to the shelter.

No one else could have heard that story before. Charlotte told me once that she had stopped talking months before they found Ruth. I wanted to tell Charlotte and Ruth, but I knew it wasn't my place.

Dad must have been thinking the same thing. "Chloe, have you told that story to anyone else?" He asked. Chloe shook her head.

"I bet your mom would like to hear that story," Dad told her.

"I'll tell her someday," she answered.

Chapter 17

When Dad and I returned home we found everyone, including Kristy, sitting at the kitchen table.

Dad walked up to Mom. "You look pale, are you okay?"

"I'm fine, just tired—it's been a long day." Mom looked thoughtful for moment. "Did you believe her story?"

"Yes, I did. A little girl couldn't make stuff like that up," he said.

"I believe her too. What a miraculous experience." Suddenly Mom jumped up and ran for the bathroom. Dad bolted after her. The bathroom was down the hall and I could hear her vomiting. Dad was right, something was wrong. I could hear voices coming from the bathroom, but I couldn't make out what they were saying. The door opened and Mom walked back into the kitchen.

"Are you okay?" Grandma asked, concerned.

"I'm fine—I just need to get some rest," Mom said.

"Do you want me to stay tonight?" Grandma asked.

"No, I'm—"

"That might be a good idea," Dad quickly cut Mom off.

"Honey no…I'm fine," Mom protested.

"I'd feel better if she's here, just in case, okay?" Dad pleaded.

"Okay," Mom gave in.

"I think I better head home," Kristy said. She grabbed her things and I walked her out. "Is your

Mom okay?"

Just then I realized I hadn't told Kristy that Mom was sick. I didn't want to tell her, either. "Yeah, she's fine," I lied. "She's just been working really hard."

Kristy smiled and I gave her a hug. She whispered to me again, "Thanks for a great day."

"You're welcome," I whispered back.

Kristy walked out into the sub-freezing temperatures. As she got to her car, she turned to wave.

Today had been great—I just hoped Mom would be okay.

I was sound asleep when Dad walked into my room and woke me up. "James, James," he said nudging me awake.

I was groggy, but awake.

"I'm taking Mom to the hospital. Grandma is here so do what she says. I'll call in the morning and let her know what's going on." I was so tired I just nodded my head and flopped back on my pillow.

Dad walked out, leaving my door open.

The phone ringing in the hallway woke me the next morning, and I heard Grandma answer it. She walked past my room and saw I was awake. "Your Mom and Dad are on their way home," she said.

As I remembered what had happened the night before, a rush of relief came over me. Everything must be fine. She wasn't there that long.

We were all downstairs eating breakfast when the door opened and Mom walked into the kitchen.

She still looked pale and tired. I looked at Dad, and I could see he was worried.

"So, what's going on?" Grandma asked.

"We'll talk about it later Mother, but for now let's eat. The doctor told me I should eat more," Mom said.

We were all eating cold cereal, but Mom decided she wanted a bowl of oatmeal. Grandma pulled a pouch out of the box and opened it, pouring hot water over the contents. Mom sat at the table with her eyes closed. She looked exhausted. I was especially worried because she said they would talk about it later. That meant she didn't want us kids to hear.

She ate all of her oatmeal, which seemed to give her a little energy. I sat down next to her. She opened her eyes and smiled. She must have seen the concern on my face, "Now, don't you worry about me, James. I'll be better by tomorrow. After school your father and I are going shopping to buy Chloe a new coat for Christmas—we want you to help pick it out."

I thought that was a great idea. Chloe would be so excited to have a coat of her own. But then I thought of the shoelaces. "What about shoelaces? She wanted shoelaces," I said.

"I think her mom will get her those. She needs a coat and I don't think her mom can afford one. She should be able to cover the shoelaces," Mom answered. Maybe Mom was right. I did tell Charlotte that Chloe asked for them.

Mom walked over to sofa and almost instantly fell asleep. Grandma shooed us all away to the game room. Nate was kicking my butt on the video game. I could hear Grandma and Dad talking and I wondered what they were talking about. I knew I shouldn't eavesdrop, but I really wanted to know what was going on. I decided to sneak down the hall to see if I could hear. "Mitchell, your turn," I told him.

"Awesome!" he said.

Nate wasn't as happy. "Ah c'mon, it's not fun playing him. He's too easy."

I turned to Nate and smiled. "Then let him win." There was no way Nate would let him win—he was too competitive. Nate shot me a nasty look as I hurried off.

I crept down the hall until I could hear Dad and Grandma talking. I quietly poked my head around the corner. "So the doctor said there's nothing that can be done?"

"He said at this point she has to roll with it. She will have good days and bad. They can try different meds, but they're not sure how she will react. The meds can make her feel worse. She doesn't want to do that. She just wants to take each day as it comes."

"Did the doctor say how long?" Grandma was asking. Dad didn't say anything, but I could see him crying. Grandma put her arm around him, trying to comfort him. My heart sank because right then and there I knew things were worse than I'd imagined. Mom was going to die and there was nothing that could be done.

102

Dad just shook his head and tried to talk but couldn't. They just sat and held each other. Grandma had tears streaming down her cheeks. Mom just lay there on the couch, so exhausted she slept through the whole conversation. Dad finally regained his composure. "He said it could be any time."

ANY TIME! I yelled in my head. I started to get tears in my eyes. How could she be dying? We need her! She can't be dying. I couldn't believe it, and kept thinking something would happen to fix

Mom's illness, perhaps a miracle like Chloe's—but deep down inside I didn't expect it.

When were they going to tell us kids? For once, I wished I would have just stayed in the game room. Walking back to my brothers, I dropped down onto our beanbag chair face-first and cried. I kept my face down so my brothers couldn't see or hear. I didn't want them to know. I wasn't sure how they would take it—especially Nate, a total mama's boy.

Later that night, Mom and Dad called for a family meeting—she looked much better, almost back to normal. Mom had rested most of the day. Dad had us all sit down and then announced, "We have a few things we need to talk to you about."

I felt anxious about what they were going to say, but Dad surprised me. "We want to know what you boys want for Christmas." Dad winked at me. "I already know what you want," he said to me.

Nate started on his list. He wanted more video games, a mountain bike, a pocketknife for scouts, and the list went on. I started on my list, which gave me something else to think about. A car was at the top, and the rest was pretty much accessories.

Then it was Mitchell's turn. He looked at Dad and then he looked at Mom, smiled and said, "I just want Mom to get better." The room fell silent. I felt so selfish—the way Nate was fidgeting I could tell he felt the same way too. Both Mom and Dad started to get emotional. I guess Mitchell catches on to a lot more than we give him credit for. At just eight years old he seems to be off in his own world most of the time. Mom and Dad had probably carried on several conversations in front of him thinking he wasn't paying attention.

Mom regained her composure, and hugged Mitchell, while Dad changed the subject. "Okay, we want to start a new tradition this year. On Christmas day we want to help serve breakfast at the shelter. I've made the arrangements with Ruth—and we can give Chloe her Christmas present when we go," he announced.

"That's great! Chloe will love it!" I said. I wondered how the other kids would feel about us giving

Chloe a gift, and not them. Maybe we'd have to find a private place for her to open it?

"It's settled then. We'll wake up, open gifts, and then go down to the shelter. I told Ruth to plan on us at 9 a.m." Dad said.

I wondered if Dad was going to talk about Mom next? But he just stood up and the meeting was over. That was fine with me. I looked forward to seeing Chloe on Christmas. I was excited to help Mom pick out Chloe's coat. Mom had great taste so whatever we chose, Chloe was going to love it.

Chapter 18

Christmas was two weeks away. Mom picked me up from school and we drove to the mall to find a coat. Mom looked great—she must have been having a good day because she seemed more like herself. She picked out a beautiful pink coat with brown buttons down the front.

"Now that looks warm, doesn't it?" Mom asked.

"Yes ma'am—the inside is down and has a waterproof shell," the sales clerk said.

"Good, we'll take it," Mom said, handing the clerk her credit card.

Mom had the coat gift-wrapped and we left the store. As we walked down the main corridor of the mall I could see Kristy coming my way. Mom started to smile as Kristy approached.

"Kristy, how are you?" she said warmly.

"I'm great, what are you two doing here?" Kristy answered.

"We just picked up a coat for Chloe," Mom announced, holding the coat for Kristy to see.

"Oh she's going to love it!" Kristy said. "Where are you heading now?"

"Home," Mom responded.

Kristy looked thoughtful. "James, I can take you home if you want to stay and do some shopping with me."

I didn't want Mom to feel bad, but I wanted to stay. I looked at Mom and she gave me a reassuring smile.

"Sure, I can stay," I told Kristy.

"Perfect! You can help me pick out a present for my Dad," she said.

I watched as Mom made her way down the hall—at first I didn't notice Kristy had continued on. I quickly caught up with her and slipped my hand over hers, feeling an electric shock pass through my body at her touch. I loved holding her hand!

Kristy got her shopping done and we sat down to share a milkshake in the food court. Neither of us said much until Kristy finally asked, "What's wrong with your Mom?" She obviously knew I had lied the other night when I'd told her nothing was wrong. So now I told her the truth. "She has cancer," I said.

Kristy gasped putting her hand to her mouth. "I'm so sorry James. Is she doing chemo?"

"Unfortunately chemo isn't going to work with her type of cancer," I said.

Kristy asked tearfully, "Is she going to get better?" I looked at the floor while I tried to hide my emotions. I didn't need everyone in the food court to see me cry. I finally shook my head. Kristy put her arm around me.

"Do they know how long she has?" she asked softly.

"They haven't actually told me, but I overheard my dad talking to my grandma. He said it could be anytime—that she'll have good and bad days up to the end," I said.

"I'm so sorry James, what can I do?" Kristy asked.

"Nothing," I shrugged my shoulders. "There isn't anything anyone can do."

Kristy didn't respond. Instead, she gave me the biggest shock of the week—of the month—of my life. She leaned over and touched her lips to mine. My mind exploded and my brain was screaming, my first kiss! I thought the electricity running through my body couldn't get any more intense than when we held hands. I was wrong—this far surpassed holding hands.

We smiled at each other for a few minutes until Kristy noticed the time. "I'm late, I have to get home," she said. We walked hand in hand to the parking lot. I opened her door for her and then walked around to get in the passenger seat. While we waited for the car to warm up, I reached over and covered her hand with mine. I didn't want this day to end.

"Thanks for the ride," I said as we got close to my house. "I hope you don't get in trouble for being late." I leaned over and gave her a quick kiss.

"It was worth it," Kristy replied sweetly.

I got out of the car and watched her back down the driveway. After she was out of sight I walked in to find Mom and Dad waiting in the kitchen. As they caught sight of me, they both burst out laughing.

Dad finally calmed down enough to say, "Go look in the mirror before your brothers see you." I rushed into the bathroom and flipped on the light. I was wearing a decent amount of Kristy's lip gloss.

I blushed, wondering if it had rubbed off on me at the mall. Did I walk through the mall with lip gloss all over my face? I was so embarrassed—until I thought of who put it there. I decided it was worth the embarrassment, but I didn't want my brothers to see—especially not Nate. He would never let me live it down. I quickly rubbed it off.

I walked back into the kitchen. Mom looked at me with her big smile. "So do you want to tell us about your first kiss? At least I'm assuming it's your first," she said.

"Sorry Mom, this isn't exactly a subject I want to discuss with my parents," I answered, embarrassed. "Oh c'mon James, you have to give me something. I've been waiting for this moment for a long time," Mom said.

"And what moment is that?" I asked. "The moment one of my kids has their first kiss!" Mom exclaimed. I thought about it and decided it wasn't a big deal to tell her—especially when it seemed so important to her. A responsible person is honest. I flashed a big smile—"Of course it was my first kiss! And it was great!"

Dad actually seemed proud. Mom clapped her hands together and laughed again. "Did you eat?"

Mom asked, still beaming.

"No we just shared a shake," I said.

"Just?" Dad joked.

"Ha ha, very funny," I said.

"Dessert, and then dessert." Dad was on a roll now.

"Okay that's enough," I protested.

Dad wiped the smirk off his face. "Okay, I'm done. I won't say another word."

"So what's for dinner?" I asked changing the subject.

"Dad wants to try a new Chinese restaurant down the street so we thought we would go out tonight.

Is that okay with you?" Mom asked.

"Sure, that sounds great!" I said. And it will be nice for Mom to have a night off from cooking, I thought.

"Get your brothers then. Let's go before it gets too late."

As I walked to the game room to tell Nate and Mitchell we were leaving, I thought of the day's events—especially the kiss. I didn't think I could ever forget the kiss.

Chapter 19

It was one week before Christmas. Dad and I had been looking at cars and I was more excited than ever. Mom and Dad went shopping almost every night, leaving me at home with my brothers. Then, after we were asleep, they would wrap the presents they had purchased and put them under the tree. It was all I could do to keep Mitchell from snooping when Mom and Dad were away.

I was still spending a few days a week at the shelter. Chloe was still talking and Ruth continued to tell me how proud she was of me for helping her. I always had to remind her it was Mom that had

helped Chloe start talking. Ruth said it would have never happened if it wasn't for me—that made me

feel really good.

Later that day, I was playing the Bunny Adventures game with Chloe in the shelter's rec room. I was trying my hardest, but she was kicking my butt. Jamal had found a new best friend to play Ping-Pong with. He didn't ask me to play anymore because I still beat him every time.

"James!" I heard Ruth's voice—she sounded stressed. I turned to see her rushing toward me.

"James, your dad will be here in five minutes. He wants you to be ready to go."

"But it's only seven. I have another hour—"

"Come on, let's go," Ruth said insistently.

I looked at Chloe and shrugged. "Bye, Chloe. Have a good night."

"You too, loser," she said making the shape of an L on her forehead. I hoped she was referring to my lousy gaming skills! Before I left, she shot me a smile that let me know she was teasing.

As I was putting on my coat Dad pulled up at the curb. I got in, and he sped off before I could even get my seat belt on. "What's going on?" I asked, becoming anxious

Dad didn't answer. That wasn't good. I thought I saw a tear in the corner of his eye. I figured it was

Mom. I hoped she was okay. When Dad pulled into the hospital parking lot my heart sank. He got out of the car and walked so quickly I had to jog to keep up. We went into the main entrance and up the elevator to the fourth floor. When the doors opened, he hurried out and I was right behind him. He walked down to room 418. Grandma was there in a chair next to the bed, crying softly. Grandpa was standing next to her, and Nate and Mitchell were sitting on the bed near Mom.

Dad walked over and took Mom's hand. I stood next to the bed. Mom's skin was gray and she had a bruise on her arm where it looked like they had taken blood. Her eyes were closed and she was having difficulty breathing. I couldn't believe how different she looked from when I had seen her this morning. Mom opened her eyes and looked at me. A slight smile slid across her lips. "James," she

said in a soft, raspy voice. "I love you, James."

"I love you too, Mom," I choked.

"James," she repeated. She was tired and it was obvious she was fighting to keep her eyes open. I looked at Dad. "She was fine this morning. What happened?" My emotions were starting to get the best of me.

"She started to go downhill after you left for school. I thought she was just tired, but she started throwing up again. I decided to bring her in. She's gotten steadily worse. The doctor told me to get you and your brothers—" Dad started to cry.

"Spence," Mom said quietly. He leaned down to her so he could hear her. "Spence, I love you."

"I love you too, sweetheart." He laid his head on her chest. She started to stroke his hair with her hand. "Stay with us Jan," Dad pleaded quietly. Mom smiled at Dad. "You know I can't, Spence."

Tears streamed down his face. "Spence," Mom said.

"Yes, honey?" Dad whispered.

"Be happy. Take care of the boys," Mom said.

"You don't have to worry about that," Dad choked. "You know I will."

"I know." Mom's breathing became shallow and her eyes slowly shut. In a few seconds, she opened them again, looked straight at Dad and whispered, "I love you."

She closed her eyes again. Her breathing became labored for several more minutes, and then, it stopped. Dad gripped her hand as the monitor went flat. Dad clasped her hand with both of his, placing it over his eyes as tears streamed down his face.

Mom was gone. My heart suddenly felt an emptiness I'd never known. I couldn't believe she was gone. Her body lay lifeless on the bed. Dad looked up as Dr. Lewis walked into the room.

"I'm so sorry Spencer. I wish there was something we could have done," Dr. Lewis said.

"Thank you doctor. You were amazing with her. She loved you." Dad shook his hand.

A nurse joined them. "Do you need help with the arrangements?" she asked Dad.

"No, they have all been made. I just have to call the funeral home," Dad said wearily.

The arrangements were made? Mom and Dad were expecting this? They knew this was going to happen so soon? At first I was upset that they hadn't told us more—but at the same time, I wouldn't have wanted to know. I was just grateful for the time I was able to spend with Mom.

Christmas was coming soon, but I didn't care anymore. I didn't care about anything—not the car or the gifts. I would give everything up in a heartbeat to have Mom back.

Chapter 20

The sun was shining and the air was crisp. December was always a cold month, and this year was no exception. There was a haze hanging over the valley, but nothing close to as thick as the haze that hung over our hearts.

The funeral was beautiful. Several people spoke and said wonderful things about Mom. Mom had touched the lives of so many people and they were all there. Seeing everyone made me want to be a better person. I wanted to live up to Mom's expectations.

Christmas was just two days away. It was heart-wrenching that she passed away so close to

Christmas, but it seemed appropriate for it to happen around the time of Christ's birth because of the way she lived her life and the sacrifices she made. She was a true Christian.

I was standing in front of her casket as Dad said a prayer before they placed it in the ground. Dad said in his prayer that her gravesite would be a place of refuge—a place where people could come to celebrate her life. I thought he said it perfectly.

Ruth brought Charlotte and Chloe. Chloe didn't say much. She'd had a special bond with Mom since Thanksgiving. I thought back to all the special experiences Chloe had brought to our family. It was almost as if Chloe was placed in our lives to help us get through this difficult time. Kristy was there to support me, but also to say goodbye to Mom.

The time had come to go home. Dad didn't want to leave Mom, but he didn't have a choice. We all felt empty inside. As we walked toward our car, Chloe ran over to us. She grabbed my hand and pulled on my arm. I knelt down so I was looking directly into her eyes. She had been crying.

"You know that picture you have of Jesus at your house?" she asked.

"Yes, Chloe, of course," I answered.

She blinked and a tear fell out onto her cheek. She then said something I'll remember for the rest of my life: "She is with Him."

Keeping with tradition, Grandma and Grandpa came over to spend Christmas Eve with us. I usually was so excited for Christmas, but my heart just wasn't in it this year. A few days ago, I asked

Charlotte if Chloe could come over. She thanked me, but said they already had plans. Chloe looked disappointed and I wondered what plans she could possibly have? I was really hoping to have Chloe with us—especially now.

Kristy said she would stop by after she had Christmas Eve with her grandparents. I hoped she would. I'd bought her a bracelet at the mall. She had pointed it out the day we were there together and Mom had taken me to pick it up a few days later.

Chapter 21

Christmas Eve at our house was gloomy. Mom was the one that had always made it exciting.

Grandma tried, but it just wasn't the same. We had dinner, but I couldn't eat much. I wasn't hungry anymore. Everything in our house, every Christmas decoration, especially the tree, reminded me of

Mom. At the funeral, I'd overheard one of Dad's friends telling him, "Time heals all wounds." I wondered if that was true—but at that moment, it seemed impossible.

Mitchell and Nate went to bed on time. Mitchell didn't want Santa to miss our house. Dad sat in his recliner, staring off into space. The way he stared blankly at the wall reminded me of the first time I had seen Chloe. The fact that she was doing so much better now gave me some feeling of hope for us.

Once Grandma was convinced my brothers were asleep, she asked if I wanted to help play Santa.

Dad got up long enough to get all the presents out of hiding using a list Mom had made for him. I wondered if she had known she wouldn't be here? She'd prepared as if she did.

Most of the gifts were wrapped and sitting next to the tree, but there were still a few last-minute purchases still waiting to be wrapped. Grandma asked Dad to get the wrapping paper. He had to use the list to find that also. Grandma handed me scissors and paper. I started to wrap the first present when I heard a soft knock on the front door. I got up and looked out the window. Kristy's car was in the drive. I quickly opened the door and let her in. A blast of cold air came in with her.

"Merry Christmas," she said.

"Merry Christmas to you too," I said softly, giving her a hug.

"How is everyone doing?" she asked.

"Okay, I guess. It's hard." It was all I could do not to cry. I was better off not talking about it.

Dad walked into the foyer to see who was here. He saw Kristy and his face brightened.

"Merry Christmas, Kristy," he said warmly.

"Thank you Mr. Miller, you too," Kristy said.

Dad returned to his recliner—only this time he picked up a book to read instead of staring at the wall.

Kristy pulled a gift from her pocket and handed it to me. "This is for you," she said. I quickly opened the box to find a watch from the same jewelry store as her bracelet. I'd seen the watch and pointed it out to her. "Thank you so much! I love it!" I gave her another hug. I walked to the tree and retrieved her present. She opened it and was surprised to see the bracelet. "It looks like we shopped at the same store!" she said.

I chuckled and asked her if she wanted to stay for a while.

"No, I don't want to intrude—besides it's getting late," she said.

"Oh, stay and help us," Grandma said. "We're wrapping a few more presents for the other boys. I can take you in the other room and you can wrap James' gifts."

Kristy pulled out her cell phone and sent a text message to her mom. Within a few minutes she had permission to stay, "I have an hour," she said.

"Perfect. It shouldn't take that long," Grandma said, walking with her into the other room. I started going through the boxes in front of me and came across a box that didn't have any markings. I opened it and inside was the coat Mom had bought for Chloe. I picked it up and walked over to Dad.

"Are we still going to help out at the shelter tomorrow?" I asked.

"You know James, I've been thinking about that. What do you think?" Dad answered.

"Did you commit to Ruth?" I asked using the words he said to me a few weeks ago.

"I told her we would be there but I—" Dad's voice faltered.

"Hey, no excuses. You made a commitment," I said with a smile. "I say we go. Besides, I think Mom would have wanted us to go, and we still need to give Chloe her coat."

Dad smiled—something I hadn't seen him do for a few days. "Okay, we'll go," he agreed.

I was excited. I couldn't wait for Chloe to see the coat. She was going to be thrilled! Just then Kristy walked in from the other room, with a big smile.

"I know what you're getting for Christmas," she said in a teasing voice.

"Tell me," I demanded playfully.

Dad sat up and said, "No!"

We both laughed. Now I had two things to look forward to—visiting Chloe and opening my gifts.

Chapter 22

I heard voices outside my door. Nate and Mitchell were fighting over who had to wake me up. I looked at the clock—6:45 on Christmas morning. I figured if we wanted to be at the shelter by nine

I'd better get up. I joined my brothers in the hall. We walked down the stairs and sat around the tree.

Grandma and Grandpa were already awake. Mitchell reached for a gift.

"Wait Mitchell, your dad is getting his camera," Grandma said.

Mitchell pulled his hand back, but it was all he could do to not grab his gifts. A few minutes later

Dad came walking in.

"Merry Christmas boys!" he exclaimed.

"Merry Christmas Dad," we all said in unison.

Dad and Grandma handed out the gifts. Pretty much everything under the tree was either for Nate or

Mitchell. They took turns opening their presents and it looked like they'd gotten most everything on their lists. Wrapping paper was strewn everywhere, and after what seemed like just minutes, all the gifts had disappeared from beneath the tree. I hadn't opened a single present and there wasn't anything left. I felt a little hurt.

Dad looked at me and smiled. "James, you didn't get anything."

I looked at him expectantly.

"Except for one thing. This year your mom and I are giving you one gift and one gift only," he said.

"This gift is because you held up your end of the bargain. You have proven yourself to be responsible, and we are proud of you." It was strange to hear him refer to Mom as if she were there.

It made sense though—they were in on this together. Dad handed me a small box.

I slowly unwrapped the paper and opened the box. Inside was a single key—a car key!

"You bought me a car?" I exclaimed, still not quite believing what I was holding in my hand.

"We pick it up tomorrow. It's all ready to go," Dad said.

I was ecstatic! My own car! I felt a little guilty for being so happy, but I was excited. My own car!

Dad smiled. Grandma and Grandpa said something about me being spoiled, but I didn't care. This was the best gift ever!

"We'd better get going if we're going to be to the shelter on time," Dad said looking at the clock.

Grandma and Grandpa wished us a Merry Christmas and headed home. The rest of us piled in

Dad's car and headed for the shelter. I was so excited to give Chloe her coat. There weren't many other cars on the road so the ride to the shelter was quick. As we pulled up to the shelter, I could see

Ruth standing in the doorway. It was cold, but she was still waiting for us, and I waved as we pulled up. Ruth smiled as we walked toward her.

"Merry Christmas!" she called.

"Merry Christmas Ruth!" we called back.

"James, Spencer—can I talk to both of you for a moment?" she asked.

"Of course," Dad replied. "Is something wrong?"

"Nothing's wrong—in fact it's a good thing. It's just going to be kind of a shock, and maybe disappointing," Ruth said. I didn't like the sound of that. What could she possibly be talking about?

"Let me explain." She pulled an envelope from her pocket. "Charlotte and Chloe are gone."

"Gone?" I was shocked. "Where did they go?"

"Charlotte was accepted into a housing program. She applied several months ago and they just got the news yesterday," Ruth said.

"Yesterday? Why couldn't she have waited one day before she left?" I was devastated. I didn't even get the chance to give Chloe the coat from Mom. I didn't get a chance to say goodbye.

"Unfortunately that's not how it works. When you get the call you have to go or risk the spot going to someone else," Ruth explained.

"Well, where is the house?" I demanded. I figured we could take the coat to Chloe wherever she was.

"I don't know that either. They don't tell me where my people are placed," Ruth said. I couldn't believe it. I was angry and I really wanted to punch something. It's a good thing Nate wasn't within arm's-length.

"James, Charlotte wrote you a note. She wanted me to give it to you." Ruth handed me the envelope she had in her hand and I took it from her. "James" was printed on the front. I tore it open to read:

Dear James,

When you read this we will be gone. I'm sure Ruth explained to you what happened. I am sorry we can't say goodbye, but I have to take this opportunity. This is our chance at a normal life.

We've been on the streets for too long. I want you to know how thankful I am that God put you into our lives. You helped Chloe more than you will ever know. She loves you and your family. She loved your mom so much. Thank you so much for all you have done for us. We will try to contact you when we get settled.

Your friend, Charlotte

P.S. Chloe got shoelaces for Christmas. They were her only gift. I hope I can give her more next year. I also wanted you to know she insisted on giving them away to someone else she cared about.

It was the only thing she had to give.

The letter comforted me a little. "We got her a coat for Christmas," I told Ruth.

"I have no way of getting it to her," Ruth said, dismayed.

"Can someone here use it?" Dad asked.

Ruth brightened. "Of course, I'll find a good home for it."

"Then we'll leave it with you, Ruth. Where would you like us to help this morning?" Dad asked.

Ruth smiled. "We're serving Christmas breakfast—ham and eggs. We'd love it if all of you could help serve. We don't get a lot of volunteers on Christmas morning." Ruth gave everyone aprons and we went to our stations. Ruth took Mitchell to the rec room to play with the other kids.

We served breakfast for a solid hour before the line died down. When we were finished serving, we took off our aprons and handed them back to Ruth. Dad asked me to get Mitchell from the rec room. When we returned, Ruth walked us to the curb and thanked us for our help. I was still disappointed Chloe was gone. I wanted to at least say goodbye, and now there was no way to find her.

Dad started the car and turned on the heater. He didn't pull out into the street right away, waiting for a moment to let the engine warm up. I was really missing Mom, but I didn't say anything. Dad finally pulled the car away from the curb, but started down a different road. He clearly wasn't going home. I didn't recognize anything until we reached the cemetery.

"I thought we should visit Mom on Christmas," he announced quietly. He wasn't going to get an argument from me—it was like Dad had read my mind.

Chapter 23

The cemetery was huge, with different roads and trails leading every which way. Dad wound his way through and parked in front of the row where Mom was buried. We all piled out of the car, put on our coats, and walked toward Mom's grave. The fresh snow crunched under our feet. Dad had purchased a large headstone for her grave, and as we approached, we could see something on it. I couldn't tell what it was until we were standing right in front. There, draped over the headstone, was a pair of bright pink shoelaces.

I knew immediately where they had come from.

"Do you think they belonged to Chloe?" Dad asked. As I looked closer I could see three bunnies printed on the laces.

"Definitely Chloe," I said. I pulled the letter from Charlotte out of my pocket and handed it to Dad.

As he read the letter, he started to cry.

"She gave her only gift to Mom," Dad said between sobs.

In that moment I realized how selfish I had been. I really was a spoiled rotten brat. As I looked at Chloe's shoelaces, I felt guilty for getting anything for Christmas. From the first minute Chloe had met Mom, she had recognized her for the wonderful person she was. On the other hand, I had lived my entire life with

Mom and didn't realize what a Christ like person she was until a few weeks ago.

Suddenly, I missed them both. I wished Mom could be here—I wished she could be here for

Christmas. Those shoelaces represented so many things to me—sacrifice, humility, and unconditional love. I thought about Chloe, Ruth, Mom and Dad, and the their lives. I thought about Jesus too. Chloe clearly knew Him and He watched out for her. I guess He watches out for all of us—sometimes He just uses other people. A powerful feeling suddenly came over me and I decided it was my turn to do something Jesus would want me to do for someone else. I looked at Dad.

"Have you paid for the car yet?" I asked.

He glanced at me, confused. "No, the check is written out, but it's sitting on my desk at home."

"I don't want you to buy the car Dad. I think I would rather you use the money to make a donation to the Family Safe Haven. Ruth could use it to help people who need it—way more than I need a car.

You know, the people there don't even get much soup, and there were probably a lot of kids who didn't get a Christmas present," I said.

Dad looked stunned. I don't think he ever imagined his test of my responsibility would have had this result. "Are you sure?" he asked, surprised.

"Yes, I'm sure. But I want the donation to be in Mom's name—to honor her memory," I added.

"She would be so proud of you right now," Dad said, his voice quiet and hoarse. "I'm proud of you James." I liked hearing Dad say that. I thought maybe this could count as my gift to Mom and to Chloe.

"Thanks Dad. I don't mind taking the bus—I have all the routes memorized now anyway," I said earnestly.

"Well James, we still have a deal. You have proven, and continue to prove, that you are extremely responsible. You can drive Mom's car for now," Dad said. I wasn't expecting to hear that, but it sounded good to me. In fact, I thought I would like driving her car more than a new one—it would be like she was with me. And I knew just what I would hang on the rearview mirror—a pair of shoelaces to serve as a reminder. I hoped I might be able to show them to Chloe someday.

I looked up at the sky. The sun cast bright warmth through the crisp winter air, and I could almost picture Mom smiling down at us. As we walked away, in fact, I felt certain she was. I gently touched the shoelaces and said a silent prayer for Chloe and Charlotte as Dad, my brothers, and I headed back to the car.

That Christmas changed my life. Even though I thought a car was the greatest gift I could ever ask for, I got something even better that year, something that has stayed with me ever since. The everlasting gift I received that year, from Dad, Mom, Ruth, and Chloe, is a reminder every holiday season that Christmas isn't about getting—it's about giving, sacrificing, and living the kind of life that inspires others to do the same.

Made in United States
North Haven, CT
19 October 2022